P9-DUZ-368

TANG IS NOT JUICE

To the Hayward Library— Bon appétit! Thanks, Vinnie Hansen

TANG IS NOT JUICE

Vinnie Hansen

Published by Mainly Murder Publishing

Tang is Not Juice

Copyright 2005 by Vinnie Hansen

All rights reserved under international and Pan-American Copyright
Conventions. No part of this book may be reproduced in any manner
whatsoever without written permission except in the case of brief
quotations embodied in critical articles or reviews. For information
address Vinnie Hansen at: vinnie@vinniehansen.com

This is a work of fiction. While some real locations have been used, I
have taken liberties. Charlie Hong Kong, for instance, didn't come to
occupy the hot dog stand until after the time of this story. Harbor View
Estates does not exist. There is a housing tract in its location. While
the problems in residential care depicted in this book are very real,
Santa Cruz County has many fine facilities that offer care to the elderly.
All the characters and incidents in this work are products of the
author's imagination. Any resemblance to actual persons, living or
dead, or actual events is entirely coincidental.

Cover design by Dragonworld Designs
Author photo by Daniel S. Friedman
Manufactured in the United States of America

ISBN 1-890625-21-3

In memory of my sister, Cecile Marie Klassen, RN

"Hansen's sense of humor and protagonist make for a good read. I particularly enjoyed her faithfully rendered Santa Cruz background."
—Laura Crum
author of the Gail McCarthy murder mystery series

"The pacing of Hansen's story is excellent." —Chris Watson
Santa Cruz Sentinel on *Murder, Honey*

"I just finished *Murder, Honey* and I found it splendid."
—Laura Davis
author of *Courage to Heal*

"With edgy precision, Hansen applies all the elements of a good mystery: interesting plot, compelling characters, a finely drawn sense of place, and excellent writing. *One Tough Cookie* has made me a fan." —Denise Osborne
author of Feng Shui Mysteries and Queenie Davilov Mysteries

"In Sabala, Hansen has created a likable sleuth whose many problems readers may readily identify with, and as far as Carol's mother goes—well, let's just say I hope we see more of her in the future."
—Michael Cornelius
The Bloomsbury Review

ACKNOWLEDGMENTS

For expert information about running residential care facilities, I am indebted to Janet Leon of Wesley House and Deborah Routley of Dominican Oaks. My husband, Daniel S. Friedman, a licensing analyst, supplied valuable information about Community Care Licensing, part of the California Department of Social Services. I also owe thanks to Tim Griffin, DDS; Kate Schmidt-Hopper, dental hygienist; Holly Bennett, RN; Mary Wampler, MD, MPH; Dennis Lippitt, Esq.; Gayle Ortiz of Gayle's Bakery; Al Vogan, gun expert; and Steve Vender, private investigator. My good friend Micah Keeley provided an indispensable proofreading, and world traveler and fellow teacher, Anna Citrino, is responsible for the observations on Kuwait. Finally, this book would not exist without the advice and assistance of Steve Lawton of Otter B Books.

PROLOGUE

The kitchen counter was innocuous, a sandstone Formica, empty and sterile. The toaster gleamed and the white microwave looked brand new.

A shaking hand placed on to the clean surface a vial and a syringe.

The label on the small bottle said: mivacurium chloride. The clear liquid served as a neuromuscular blocking agent, a muscle paralyzer.

Oblivious, the old bag sat in her maroon Lazyboy popping peanuts into her mouth. She acted like she was some sort of queen, but she looked like a toad. A toad about to drown in her own saliva.

CHAPTER 1

Harbor View Estates was slick. Slick marble reception counter, slick brochures, and slick sales pitch. My mom would fall for it hook, line and sinker. I groaned inwardly at my use of cliché. Cliché-ridden language was my mother's province. I was becoming more like her with each waking second; perhaps that accounted for my anxiety. I folded the brochure, and folded it again, clutching it in my damp palm. One day, like my mom, I'd be shopping for a retirement community.

"Harbor View Estates offers three tiers of service," the sales counselor chirped.

The rosy-cheeked blonde, Wendy Keegan, couldn't be more than thirty. In her mauve knit shirt with an HVE logo, she would have been more appropriate hustling spa memberships. I trailed Wendy Keegan and my mom. The hallway was not slick, but dark patterned burgundy carpet to maximize stain concealment and minimize law suits.

"We offer independent living, assisted living and a unique dementia unit," Wendy Keegan explained. "I would assume, given how great you look, that you're considering an independent living unit."

My mom nodded curtly. I resented the way Ms. Keegan was pitching my mom and dismissing me. Could she detect the negativity oozing from me? I had better ways to spend a Monday than to shop for a place to drop. To most people Happy Monday may have been the king of all oxymora, but as a baker,

I had the day off.

Mom had dolled up in black slacks, elastic-waisted. From my earliest memories, my mom had conceded style to comfort. She also wore a pink shiny blouse with long puffy sleeves and a tie, the kind of blouse a person could find nowadays only in a thrift shop.

"Our price includes all your meals, snacks, transportation to and from your doctor's office, and a wide-array of activities, the best in the area." The pretty Ms. Keegan looked the way I imagined my mom wished I did—decidedly feminine with her pearl earrings and necklace. My mom would surely be suckered in by all this.

When we had arrived at Harbor View Estates, she'd murmured at the grassy knolls and beds of pink and purple asters. "Aren't these grounds lovely?"

"Where's the harbor view?" I'd asked. Perhaps if I climbed one of the man-made knolls and cranked my head just so, I could get a glimpse of a mast. I appreciated places like Capitola Mall and the honesty of its name. Everything should be named that way. Instead of Harbor View Estates, this should be called Santa Cruz Retirement Home Number 27. "Don't you think an estate should have a little more property to it?" I'd asked my mom.

"I don't know why you're so opposed to me moving into a retirement community," my mom had mildly responded.

"I'm not opposed to it. I'm just more cynical than you are."

Now I watched my mom continue down the hall, undeterred by my cynicism. She'd grown up in rural northern California where people knew each other and helped their neighbors. She had no inkling that someone with Wendy Keegan's scrubbed clean, all-American looks could be rattling off a prepackaged, corporate, commission-based-on-sales presentation. Motivated by her need to pay her rent, the girl acted in the interests of the owners of Harbor View Estates, who had profit margins, not my mother's well-being, foremost in their minds.

When did this phenomenon occur? I wondered. When did my mom stop being my mom and become a strong-willed child? When did we switch places? When had I started to look out for her more than she looked out for me?

The decline had not started at retirement. My mother had stayed at her job as a dental hygienist far too long, and had continued part-time at the front desk of the dental office into her old age. She gardened and knitted and traveled to quilt shows. Even when she'd given up that life and moved to Santa Cruz last year, she'd still seemed spry. But who could tell what was going on inside, especially with someone like my mom? My brother Donald's death had no doubt been a blow. Seven years, and pain still stabbed into my heart at the thought of him.

Donald had been a much better son than I was a daughter. He'd visited, for one thing. Not only that, but he used the time to paint rooms, trim shrubs, and force Mom to shop for new towels. When he died, I was too devastated to notice the effect on my mom. Certainly when I'd visited, her house had become shabbier. Looking back now, it did seem she'd become more pinched and world-weary.

Ms. Keegan's black pumps padded down the hallway. I could tell that she'd prefer to be bustling along carrying a clipboard; she had to restrain her pace for my mom even though my mom was a very able-bodied senior. At seventy-five she had a dowager's hump that I blamed on years of stooping over to clean people's teeth, but other than that, she was in good form; she certainly didn't need to spend three thousand dollars a month to be in a facility.

"I'm just shopping," she'd snapped at me. "I think it's best that I do that while I am still in tact, don't you?"

"But you're perfectly healthy. You have years to do this."

Last year she had discovered that her LDL cholesterol was high and her HDL was low. Her doctor had suggested a diet and she'd lost fifteen pounds. Now I thought she looked frail and at last report she'd claimed she felt "poky." I wanted her to reassure me that she was in great health, that there was no pressing need for her to receive care. But my mom had never been the reassuring type.

"You don't have to go if you don't want to," she'd said.

Out of guilt, I plodded resentfully behind the sales counselor and my mom. I didn't want my mom to live with me and I certainly couldn't afford to pay for her care here. As a baker, I couldn't afford to help my mom out with any of her retirement needs. I felt inadequate, the way she had as a struggling single mother.

Ms. Keegan warbled on about the activities—bridge, bingo, readings, birthday celebrations, hymn sing-alongs on Sunday . . . .

One photo in the brochure showed four female residents decked out for Halloween. Once I'd wanted a store-bought, Superman costume for Halloween. I didn't have enough money and my mom wouldn't buy it. I'd been a regular shit about it, calling her a grinch. I'd thought that she didn't want me to be a tomboy, but in our financially strapped existence, she'd probably seen the outfit as frivolous.

A cherry red electric cart whirred toward us, a half dozen flags waving from poles on its rear. The crazed elderly driver seemed ready to mow us down. Beside her trotted a young woman with bleached blond hair shorn in the modern stick fashion. The tips of her ragged hair were dyed blue. She wore the required mauve shirt with its HVE logo and a black mini skirt.

"Careful, Gladys," Wendy Keegan admonished. The abrupt appearance of the two characters had clearly harshed her mellow, perhaps jeopardizing a potential sale.

Gladys stopped beside us. She was a barrel-chested, wheezy

woman with red hair. Even though she was a heavy woman and the weather was warm, she carried a crocheted throw on her lap. "Don't be such a worry wart," she snapped at Wendy. "My Pride Voyager handles like a Ferrari." Gladys sized up my mom. "Besides I have Chrissie to look after me. Don't I, honey?"

The girl stood there sullenly, scratching her arms and not acknowledging us.

I checked out the flags on the woman's cart—an American flag, one that said *Gladys* in gold satin on purple felt, one streaming tassels of silver that looked like a wand for a good fairy costume, an AARP pennant, a Giants pennant, a state of California flag, and one that said Caution: *Ornery Senior on Board.*

Wendy checked her watch. "Chrissie should be helping Nurse Motha."

A silent showdown took place between Wendy and Gladys. Even with my nearly non-existent social life, I'd encountered these moments at parties. Maybe Uncle Fred had drunk too much and was trying to torture the cat again, but neither the host nor hostess wanted to ruin anyone's good time with a shouting match about whose stupid uncle he was. Nor did they want to draw attention to the embarrassing behavior of Freddy. Instead they waged a war of silent commands.

"I'll go help Nurse Moco," Chrissie muttered. In Spanish moco meant snot. Chrissie spun and huffed off down the hall.

Wendy turned away from the elderly woman in the cart. "We have a nurse here," Wendy said, trying to put a positive spin on this little drama.

"A nurse who earns her nicknames," Gladys spit. "If it weren't for her, maybe Mildred would still be alive."

Wendy's face furrowed in irritation.

"Chrissie is a good girl," Gladys insisted.

Wendy plastered a smile on her face. "Of course she is, Gladys." She glanced back over her shoulder.

Gladys wiggled a little straighter in her cart's seat. Her green eyes sparked with indignation and she wheezed in preparation to speak.

Wendy changed her tack. "Gladys, this is Bea Sabala and her daughter, Carol."

Gladys relaxed back into the black seat. "Are you looking for a room?" she said to me with a wink.

"Maybe. I'm a whiz at bingo."

She chuckled, a gurgling, strained sound that turned into coughs. She put a hand on her chest. "The best part of this place is the young helpers like Chrissie."

The viper had decided to strike Wendy after all. She reached up and took my mom's hand. "I'm Gladys Mills."

"Pleased to meet you," my mom said, giving the hand a pump. "I was admiring your Granny Square lap rug."

Gladys's plump, freckled hand kept its hold on my mom's bony fingers. "Do you crochet?" Her green eyes sparkled.

"A little," my mom said with her usual understatement.

My mom had crocheted enough throws to carpet the annual Wharf to Wharf run.

"I used to quilt, but crochet is more portable and relaxing," my mom added.

"Isn't it though?" Gladys exclaimed, finally releasing my mom. "My friend Ida and I tried to start a Crochet and Crab Club, but the women here are the highfalutin tea and opera types. But Ida and I are both transplanted Okies. Came out here with our parents to work in the prunes and almonds."

She pronounced almonds as amends.

My mom looked as though she'd found a new best friend. Gladys Mills was perfect. Her outgoing nature a counterpoint to my mom's blunt reserve. Yet, Gladys knew hard work. My mom, who grew up on a dairy farm near Ferndale, appreciated people who understood the meaning of toil. Gladys scored further points for disliking the hoity-toity. And, the woman liked to crochet. I expected my mom to move in tomorrow.

"Listen, dear, if you come to live at this joint, or you just want the lowdown, look me up. Gladys Mills in 302. I'll tell you which guys still have all their marbles."

CHAPTER 2

I snuggled into the crook of David Shapiro's arm and played with his chest hair. He had the right amount; nothing creeping over his shoulders and down his back. He was a hot tamale under the covers, and had been well-trained by his former wife and many girlfriends to be a good cuddler.

"Is there anything about my house you like?" he asked.

My eyes roved his bedroom. I hated the foam bed and the brown shag carpet. The master bath had peeling linoleum, a shower that didn't work, and a need to be scrubbed with Lysol from ceiling to floor.

"I guess not," he said glumly, although mentally I was still walking down the hallway to the living room.

"I like the fireplace."

"Well, that's something," David said.

This was not new territory for us. Our relationship had reached an impasse. We had been dating each other exclusively for over a year and the next logical step would be to move in together.

"Is there anything you like about my house?" I asked in turn.

"It's too small," he said with finality.

"Ideally, we should buy a new house. Neutral territory."

"Ideally," he echoed.

The houses provided convenient barriers. We were both independent and opinionated. As long as we maintained separate domiciles, we could sidestep the issue of how our lives would mesh.

I'd started to see David only six months after my divorce. Even though the divorce had been my idea, it had been more painful than I'd expected, and a part of me felt like playing the field forever. My former husband had been a roofer and he'd tried to put a lid on me.

"I'm the transition relationship that won't leave," David laughingly told my friends.

He pulled himself into a sitting position, using a stack of pillows against the wall. I moved my head to his stomach. It was soft, but firm—no washboard muscles, but no flab either. He had a comfortable, compact body. He sank his hand into my thick auburn hair and scratched at my scalp. "How did it go the other day with The Mom?"

"It depressed the hell out of me."

"Was it the sight of all the walkers or the smell of adult diapers?"

I sat up. "The whole thing," I moaned, "from the sale's pitches to the idea my mom's getting old."

During the tours of facilities, I'd also discovered an unpleasant truth about myself. I feared being alone in the world. My father had deserted the family and disappeared when I was a baby and my older brother Donald had died officially from pneumonia, but really from AIDS. While I considered myself independent and often found my mom annoying, the idea of no immediate family filled me with anxiety.

"There's only one alternative to getting old," David said.

"Thanks for that cheery thought."

He laughed. The more sarcastic I was, the more he enjoyed me. In some ways, he was a perfect match. "Has anyone ever told you that when you talk, you look like you're signing for the deaf?" He waved his hands around in parody.

I ignored him and rattled off the various facilities my mom

and I had visited.

"Harbor View Estates." He whistled. "Your mom must be rolling in the dough. That place charges a four thousand dollar nonrefundable deposit."

I kissed David's shoulder. "I don't know what my mom's doing. She's very private about money. For all I know, she could have invested in Cisco."

The previous year, my mom had plopped down ten thousand dollars to help me buy out my ex-husband's interest in my house. She said it was payment for a background check I'd done, but that was ludicrous. In November, she'd followed up with a birthday present of five thousand dollars. "Don't worry," my mom had said, "I have plenty." Then she'd added in her usual, endearing way, "I'm leaving everything that's left over to you, anyway."

"That place may be fancy," I said to David, "but one of the aides I saw looked like she belonged in a heavy-metal band. She had this serpent tattoo twisting down one arm and those piercings in her ears—the kind you can stick a dime in."

"I hate those," he said emphatically.

I loved this guy. He was a lover and a best girlfriend combined.

"All those places are desperate for help," he explained. "The pay sucks. With tips, a waitress at Zachary's can make better money, and what would you rather do, work at a hip spot downtown or change diapers on wrinkly old bottoms?"

This was one of David Shapiro's litanies. He was a part-time investigator for Community Care Licensing, a branch of the California Department of Social Services. He kept me apprised of his investigations, and had set me up with one of his friends in private enterprise so that I could earn training hours towards my investigator's license as I continued to earn my bread and butter at my job as a baker.

David generally investigated allegations of abuse at state-licensed facilities. The facilities ranged from group homes for juvenile delinquents, to adult facilities for the mentally ill to old folks' homes. I'd expected his work to be more interesting than it was. After all, David owned a 38 caliber Colt Detective Special. "I've taken that out with me about twice in twenty years," he'd informed me.

As often as not, his investigations uncovered a disgruntled employee making trouble for the facility with false reports. There was no abuse, unless one counted eight dollars an hour with no benefits as abuse.

My work for David's friend, J.J. Sloan of Sloan's Investigative Services, was only slightly more interesting. My first job had been to spy on the neighbor of a wealthy eccentric. Mr. Frederick, the wealthy eccentric, our client, had a long running feud with his neighbor, a contractor. The contractor was currently building a two-story structure that would overlook the Frederick's property. The permits were for a nonhabitable building, but our client suspected the neighbor was building a granny unit. He had hired J.J. to watch the construction daily from eight to four to make sure the neighbor didn't install a toilet or both insulation and Sheetrock to make the structure habitable.

I sat up and pulled on my tee-shirt. Or was it David's? I quickly stripped off the shirt.

"Now this I like," David said.

I sniffed the shirt's armpit.

"Good thing this is not a first date."

I threw his shirt at him and fished off the side of the bed to find mine.

"I'll ask my friend Leonard about the facilities your mom is considering. For right now, I can say that I've never been called to any of them."

"That's good."

"Now what about my kitchen," he persisted. "You have to admit it's a much better kitchen than yours."

CHAPTER 3

When I arrived at my little stucco house, Lola crawled over the back fence, plopped to the ground and waddled out to greet me. Since I'd decided to let her eat as much as she liked, Lola had become contented and Rubenesque. The balmy Indian summer air kissed my skin and the palm tree rustled above me.

In my mailbox, I found a long, personal letter from my friend Suzanne Anderson. She'd gone off to Kuwait with her new found love—Hamad Marzouk. She'd needed to escape the memory of her murdered cousin, a case I'd investigated last year.

With a cup of black coffee, I settled at a round oak table that had been my grandmother's. Lola curled into my lap. I ran my fingers over the light blue airmail envelope. Sex and a personal letter—it was a banner day.

> *Dear Carol,*
> *I'm definitely having the adventure of my lifetime. I was probably the only American on the plane from Frankfurt. The passengers were mostly Arabs and Europeans and a few Indians. When we landed in Kuwait, I was impressed by the modern airport—white marble walls and pillars. The waiting room had glass walls and the airport stores were chock full of the latest electronic gadgets.*
> *The grunt work here is done by people who look Indian. Hamad hired one at the baggage terminal to*

*help us with our forty million bags. They were dressed
in florescent orange jumpsuits, unlike the Kuwaiti
people who seem to dress all in black and white. Their
dress reminds me of nun's habits. Even Hamad has a
dishdasha that he puts on to go out to the diwaniya.
That's a place where men gather. They drink tea and
smoke and shoot the shit. At least that's what Hamad
tells me. There's no drinking here. When we went
through immigration, we were asked if we had any
alcohol in our bags. We said no, but they checked
anyway, probably because I was obviously a foreigner.*

    *The heat outside was like a sledge hammer. Thank
God for air conditioning. It is just like you told me
that day you made me stand in front of the oven. There's
no soil here, just sand and a sense of vast openness.
Everything's monochrome—beige. Beige sand and beige
buildings. The country looks best at night when the
buildings are lit. When we were walking up to Hamad's
apartment, I heard the mosque call for the first time.
It's a spooky, eerie sound and I'm still not used to it. I'm
definitely sleep deprived because the damn thing sounds
every few hours.*

    *I'm more in love with Hamad than ever, and this
trip, so far, has been exciting for me. But I'll be ready
to come home sooner rather than later. Even though
Hamad's family has "wasta," a certain social and
political power, as a woman there's not much I can do
here. It's not advised that I go out on my own, so while
Hamad's out rabble rousing, I sit around and write
letters and read books.*

With her usual thoughtfulness, Suzanne went on to ask about
David, my mom, and the people in the kitchen of Archibald's,
where she had worked as garde manger, and I still worked as a

baker. Suzanne had been my best friend at work and her absence tasted like green fruit.

As I was finishing the letter, the phone rang.

Without preamble, my mom asked, "What was the name of that woman we met?"

I hated that my mom assumed I knew who she meant even though we'd recently met a half dozen women. I hated even more that I did know. "Gladys Mills."

"That's right. I kept thinking Gertrude, but I knew that wasn't right. Thank you."

"Wait a minute, Mom." She would have hung up with no further ado. "Why did you want to know that?"

"I thought I'd go visit her."

"That sounds nice. You could get the inside scoop on that place."

"I just want to get some help with my popcorn stitch. I haven't used it for a while and I'm doing something wrong."

These little things made me worry. My mom had always possessed an excellent memory—too excellent. She remembered all the things I wanted to forget. Now she'd forgotten Gladys Mills' name and how to make a common crochet stitch.

"How were you planning to get there?"

"I'll take the 71 bus. It runs right down Soquel Drive."

"It's quite a hike up that hill to the facility."

"I'll be fine."

"If you can wait until I get off work tomorrow, I'll take you."

My mom hated the idea of being a pain in the ass. Normally she would have instantly declined the offer. The lack of protest verified that she "didn't have much poop."

"I'll pick you up at two." I didn't like to admit it, but the way things looked with my mom, it might not be a bad idea to gather some inside information about Harbor View Estates.

CHAPTER 4

Gladys Mills took another inhalation from her oxygen and finished demonstrating the popcorn stitch. My mom watched Gladys carefully while I inspected the spotlessly clean, one-bedroom apartment. It smelled of pine cleaner and cigarettes.

In the kitchenette, Chrissie was unpacking a bag from Safeway. She no longer wore her mauve HVE shirt, but rather a yellow tee-shirt that said, "I like your boyfriend." It rode above the same black mini skirt we'd seen on our previous visit, revealing the top of a tattoo on her lower back.

"I've hired Chrissie as my private assistant," Gladys explained. "She's practically kin, anyway."

"Her former daughter-in-law hooked up with my dad," Chrissie clarified, not sounding too happy about the arrangement.

"Now you get to enjoy Melanie," Gladys whooped, cackled, and then coughed, leaning over her maroon Lazyboy to snort some oxygen. Her tank was small and portable and her intake slipped over her ears like glasses and up her nose. Gladys's blouse, patterned with orange hibiscus against a bold purple, clashed with her chair and her hair.

"Yeah, right," Chrissie said sarcastically. "More like dad gets to enjoy the bitch." She turned quickly to my mom. "Sorry." The belligerence in Chrissie's manner belied her thin, waif-like appearance.

"Now, now," Gladys chided the girl. "Melanie is the mother

of my grandchildren and she does have spine, staying with that no good son of mine all those years."

"Compared to some of the kids of the other residents, Rusty's pretty considerate." Chrissie's unpacking method involved lots of banging and door slamming. "He visits you every week, Gladys."

"That's because he's thirsting after my money."

Gladys had stopped crocheting quite some time ago, so my mom and I were stuck standing near her chair and listening to the family soap opera. I gazed out the sliding glass door. On the patio a wire bird feeder hung from a wrought iron rod and a ceramic bird bath was secured to the top rail. A chaise lounge with a brightly flowered cushion occupied center stage. Draped in crocheted throws, it reminded me of a queen's throne. Gladys presided over a view of Arana Gulch Open Space and the tips of the masts at the Yacht Harbor. Not bad.

"I thank you kindly," my mom interjected to Gladys, trying in her mild way to extricate herself.

"Where do you want these peanuts?" Chrissie demanded. "You're not supposed to be eating these."

"Be a good girl and put them in my dish. I suppose you think I'm supposed to eat the garbage they serve here." Gladys motioned for Chrissie to put the peanuts in a crystal bowl on the table beside her Lazyboy. "What's life if we give up our little pleasures?"

"Like these." Chrissie shook a carton of Larks at her and the serpent tattoo on her arm wriggled ominously.

"Cigarettes are one of life's big pleasures."

Chrissie scowled. Her brown eyes and nearly black brows made me guess her natural hair was dark.

My mom wrinkled her nose. I was probably wrinkling mine, too. Amazingly, I'd once been married to a smoker.

"You're going to get kicked out of here if you keep smoking in your room," Chrissie warned.

Given the oxygen tank, they both should be more concerned about Gladys blowing them to a beach front view.

"They're not going to kick me out. They get their check on time every month." Gladys adjusted the lever of her Lazyboy and pressed back into a reclining position. "I suppose you, of all people, are going to lecture me on the evils of cigarettes."

Chrissie dodged around us and smacked down one of the packages of Larks by Gladys's chair. "I never smoke cigarettes!"

"Well la dee dah. I'm sure you smoke everything else."

Out of things to say, Chrissie stood with her arms crossed, scratching at her biceps with chipped blue fingernails. Chrissie and Gladys spoke to each other in the intimate, abusive way of family even if they weren't blood relatives. It was worse than my mom and I, and not that much fun to be around.

"Thank you again, Gladys," my mom said. "That was really helpful. We should be on our way."

"You're not leaving so soon." It was more command than question. She waved at a tan love seat, and my mom, who had better manners than I had, reluctantly took a seat. "I need to give you the lowdown on this place."

Since this had been my reason for tagging along, I resigned myself to the other cushion. "Chrissie, bring us some drinks."

The girl's body straightened, more rigid than her bleached hair. I expected her to bark, "Fuck you! I'm not your slave." Instead, she simply glared at me and my mom and said, "Nothing alcoholic."

My mom gave Chrissie a mournful, basset-hound look. My mom, for all intents and purposes, was a teetotaler, and the very notion she'd order a cocktail in the mid-afternoon was offensive.

"Dang," I said. "I had my heart set on a very dry martini with onions."

Chrissie gave me a tight ha-ha-very-funny smile.

"What would you ladies like?" Gladys said with largess.

I ordered black coffee for myself and a cup of tea for my

mom. My mom shot me daggers which was exactly why I'd ordered her some tea. She had every intention of politely listening to this woman, for God knew how long, without affording herself any sustenance. At the moment she looked a little peaked, but maybe that was the reflection from her white blouse.

"Make that tea with some cream and sugar," I told Chrissie.

"Does your mom need real sugar?"

"No," Mom said.

"Yes, she does." In spite of all her years working in a dentist's office, my mom loved sugar and sweets. I'd never seen her use artificial sweetener in her life, and I wasn't going to let her do so now. Besides, I didn't mind causing Chrissie some inconvenience.

She heaved a sigh. "I'll have to go to the cafeteria for that."

What pressing engagement do you have that makes that a problem? I thought.

The young woman flounced out the door, pulling her purse off the door knob.

"You have to excuse Chrissie," Gladys said.

I do not, I thought. If I were a gambling woman, I'd bet people had been making excuses for Chrissie most of her life.

"She's always had her daddy wrapped around her little finger, and now he's wrapped around Melanie's. She's been taking it pretty hard."

"She seems old enough to cut the umbilical cord," my mom said curtly.

I felt like leaning over and planting a big wet one on her withered cheek. Forget all the make-nice, coconut custard filling, underneath my mom was pure crust.

Gladys pursed her lips. Unlike my mom, she wore makeup—lipstick, blush, and mascara, and her plump face retained a creaminess. "Well, that's probably true," Gladys finally said, "but I've known Chrissie all her life and she has had problems since the day she was born. Shoot. I've known her daddy, Michael Locatelli, all his life."

The name Michael Locatelli rang a bell, but I couldn't place it.

"When Mike was young, he was wild, too. That's why he has a twenty-one-year-old daughter born out of wedlock. Who would have ever thought he'd settle down? Especially with someone like Melanie, who's already been married and has kids. Of course, she is a looker."

And Michael Locatelli was getting old and probably going bald.

"What would you say is the biggest drawback to Harbor View Estates?" I asked abruptly. Gladys seemed self-involved and capable of prattling ad infinitum.

My mother looked quite pale and I wondered how long it took to trot down to the cafeteria and back.

"Well," Gladys eyed the cigarettes, but settled for a handful of salted peanuts, "the best things are the rooms." Like Ed Sullivan introducing a guest, she gestured majestically at her apartment and stuffed her mouth. She knew damn good and well that she hadn't answered my question.

She finished chewing and turned in her chair to address my mom. "Are you all right, Bea? You look all tuckered out."

If you hadn't kept her standing for twenty minutes, she wouldn't look so white, I thought angrily.

"I'm fine," my mom said.

"Have some peanuts," Gladys said.

"No, thank you."

"We're mainly interested in the negative," I said bluntly. "The things the sales counselor won't point out."

"Well, Wendy won't tell you that Jack Dorfman's a lout and Nurse Motha's a sadist."

"Who's Jack Dorfman?" I asked.

"An old geezer in room 606. An ass grabber."

"Is he a dementia patient?"

"Oh no. He doesn't have any screws loose in that way. He

knows exactly what he's doing."

"How about Nurse Motha? What's the story there?"

"She hates old people."

"Why does she work here?"

"Contrary to what the sales rep would like you to believe, she's from VNA."

"VNA?" I asked.

"Visiting Nurse Association. She's a traveling nurse. She works a lot of places."

"Why would a place as ritzy as this take someone who doesn't like the elderly?"

"Truth be told, they don't have a nurse at all. Nurse Motha is not on staff. She's hired by a group of residents and their families. They're basically doing what I'm doing with Chrissie. These places are always short staffed. I don't have the patience to deal with things like delayed room cleaning because the maid quit-again."

I wondered how long Chrissie would last given that she still had not returned with the sugar.

"Have you ever considered changing to another facility?" my mom asked.

"No. I like this apartment and my good friend Ida Walker lives here. Two doors down. 306. You should stop and say hi to her, Bea. Now that woman can knit and crochet. You should see her crewelwork. She even does tatting."

How could a woman who needed an oxygen tank yak so much. I cleared my throat. "Problems with the facility?" I prompted.

"We just got a new administrator, Katherine O'Conner. I'm optimistic about her. I'm also fortunate enough to be able to work around this place's shortcomings."

"Like the sadistic nurse?" I asked.

"Excuse me," my mom said, trying to push up out of the love seat, "I think we better head along."

I stood in time to catch my mom as she collapsed.

Gladys ejected from her Lazyboy, glided across the room in a walker, and yanked a cord by her bathroom shower.

CHAPTER 5

Nurse Motha responded promptly to Gladys's emergency alert. She huffed into the room, a big, bulky woman, strong from years of hefting patients. Even though my mom's eyes had fluttered open, the nurse quickly loosened the top button of my mom's blouse, raised her knees up over the end of the love seat and ordered me to prepare a cold compress.

Since I'd choose competence over a good bedside manner any day, Nurse Motha didn't seem like a sadist to me. More like an angel of mercy; she wasn't even employed by the facility, but here she was. With fluffy blond hair, blue eyes, and rosy cheeks, her face looked like Western culture's idea of an angel.

"You fainted," she explained to my mom as she listened to her heart and took her blood pressure.

The new administrator Katherine O'Conner made an appearance. She was a forty-something woman in a turquoise business suit. Her face was preternaturally smooth and the flip in her honey-colored hair looked stiff enough to hold salsa.

"Is everything okay?" she asked the nurse. When she spoke, her face didn't move. I suspected Botox treatments which worked by paralyzing facial muscles, thus eliminating the lines of expression that made us look human.

The nurse nodded.

"Chrissie is supposed to be getting some sugar for her tea. That should buck her up."

"Chrissie?" the administrator asked.

"My personal assistant," Gladys admonished.

Chrissie chose that moment to show up with the coffee and tea. She'd prepared the drinks in the cafeteria which partially explained why she'd taken twenty minutes. My mom sat up, sipped the tea, and regained some color.

The administrator squatted before my mom and murmured reassurances that sounded like *please be okay because I just started my job and lawsuits are career enders.*

Gladys asked for my mom's number so that she could check on her later. I wrote my mom's name and number on a notepad by her chair. "Here's mine, too," I said. It seemed like the right thing to do even though I hoped the woman never called me.

I used Gladys's phone to call my mom's doctor to see if he could squeeze her in before closing up shop.

I hadn't asked anyone permission to come into the examining room. I'd simply followed my mom and neither she nor anyone else had asked me to leave. A phlebotomist had drawn her blood and a nurse had taken her blood pressure and asked her a few questions. Now the doctor had arrived.

Doctor Jellinek was a short man with tightly curled red hair and a hawkish nose. Even though he exuded intelligence and had a sense of humor, he was the one who had recommended the Pravachol to lower my mom's cholesterol which had resulted in the fifteen pound weight loss. I felt a little hostile toward him.

The vaguely pink cupboards featured a notice that cell phone usage was not allowed in the examining room. "It's amazing that you have to post that notice," I said.

"Truly," Doctor Jellinek replied. "I came in once and this guy talking on his phone gave me one of these." The doctor held up an outward facing index finger. "I gave him one of these." The doctor held up five fingers and waved bye.

"Well, young lady," he said to my mom, "it would seem

that you have become quite anemic." In addition to the usual advice about diet, he prescribed another drug, meant to help her blood absorb nutrients.

As I drove my mom home, I suggested that we stop somewhere to eat. I had in mind a juicy red steak for her.

"Let's try Charlie Hong Kong."

Asked two years ago, I would have said that my mom was strictly a Denny's-type diner, but since she'd moved to Santa Cruz, a whole new side of her had emerged. Her former eating habits may have been determined by lack of opportunity rather than personal taste. Context does define us. People we've seen a hundred times, out of context, are suddenly unfamiliar.

Maybe one did need a radical shift in place to see one's self in a new way. That had been Suzanne's argument for going to Kuwait.

"I need the roughage," my mom explained.

Charlie Hong Kong had once been a hot dog stand. It may have been tiny, but it featured The World's Most Confusing Parking Lot. I maneuvered my Ghia into the L-shaped lot. That was the easy part. The problem was leaving. The lot had two entrances and no exit.

The food began with fresh noodles and built from there. At the window, my mom ordered Laughing Phoenix Red Curry and I ordered Charlie's Pad Thai with a chicken topping.

"Don't you work at Archibald's?" an astounded voice asked.

I turned around to stare at an unfamiliar, middle-aged woman. "I'm the baker."

"That's right!" she exclaimed. "I love your croissants."

This happened to me every now and then. A person at a Sunday brunch may have seen me delivering a basket of scones to the tables and chatted me up about my creations. Later the person would be flabbergasted to see me eating at McDonald's, as though a baker at a place like Archibald's lived on caviar and paté.

"Inside or out?" I asked my mom. Our choices were exterior picnic tables or the counter circling the perimeter of the minuscule lobby. We sat looking out at the traffic on Soquel Drive.

"I'd like to take Gladys and that nurse a little something," my mom said. "What do you think? Flowers or candy or what?"

I did not want to visit Gladys Mills again, but I couldn't let my mom take the bus and climb a half mile hill after she'd passed out. So I tried to convince her it was okay to be thankless. "Look, mom, all you did was faint. What were they going to do, leave you on the floor? It's a nurse's job to look after people."

"I'm not one of her customers," my mom snapped. "She isn't paid to look after me."

Our number was called and I was happy to spring up to get the meals. If my mom was going senile, maybe she'd forget her plan while I was gone.

But she wasn't distracted even by the arrival of the vegetables in tomato-coconut sauce garnished with cilantro and scallions. "Don't worry, Carol. You don't have to haul me around. If I think the walk will be too draining, I'll take a taxi rather than the bus. I just wondered what might make an appropriate gift."

From my former mother-in-law, these machinations would have been meant to guilt-trip me into a ride. Her manipulations would have made me angry and able to resist her. My mother meant exactly what she'd said. She'd take a taxi. No problem. For some perverse reason, her independence worked on my conscience like the tomato-tamarind sauce worked on my taste buds.

"Look, I'm going on a bike ride with David tomorrow, but if you wait until Saturday, I'd *like* to drive you over there."

She was definitely in a weakened condition. She didn't even argue.

CHAPTER 6

David unloaded the bikes behind the fire station on the University of California campus. He'd convinced me to upgrade my fifteen-year-old Schwinn three speed to a Trek 820 with a Manitou elastemer shock, an introductory mountain bike. As we put on our gloves and helmets, he resumed the argument of two days ago. "You must like the hot tub at my house."

"I love the hot tub."

I took off up the fire road behind the station. The short, steep climb guaranteed a break in the conversation.

David was dissatisfied with the status quo of our relationship. In truth, I was dissatisfied, too. The constant transporting of underwear and hairbrush. The neglect of my little yard and Lola. But I didn't want to give up a house I'd bought only a year ago.

The dirt and gravel road plumed dust, dry from the summer and hot September days. Even though I was out of breath, I didn't wait for David at the top. The sun filtered through the redwoods and the silence enveloped me.

Patellar tendonitis had ended my volleyball playing and I felt glad that David had badgered me into mountain biking. I missed the camaraderie of a team, but liked the Zen experience of focusing on a trail.

Redwood duff muffled the sound of David rapidly overtaking me. "You could rent your house," he said, as though he'd been following my thoughts. "If things don't work out, you could move back."

"I don't like the idea of being a landlady."

"I'll help. I've been a landlord before."

That was part of the problem. David had done so many things. He'd been divorced most of his adult life. He'd raised a son, traveled the world, and developed his hobby of photography to an art form and a source of income. Everything I mentioned, he'd been there, done that. Or he implied that he had. He had an exuberant, assertive personality that wasn't beyond embellishing. If I lived with him, I'd be overshadowed. "Let's talk about something else."

"Harbor View Estates is part of Leonard's caseload and he had some interesting things to say about it."

"Tell me." The fire road rolled easily through the pine and redwoods. We were completely alone with the cawing jays. When I wasn't busy moonlighting for J.J. Sloan's Investigative Services, I loved the way my job as a baker allowed weekdays off.

"Harbor View receives a lot of complaints."

"What kind of complaints?"

"Leonard says it runs the whole gamut. A lot of them are unsubstantiated. With a facility like that, the sons and daughters tend to be well-educated and to feel guilty about shunting their mom or dad into a facility. They complain about the least little thing."

"So it's basically a good place?"

"Nah. Leonard says it sucks. He was out there once and their menu said juice, but they were serving Tang. He wrote in his report: Tang is not juice." David laughed. He pedaled his aluminum-framed Trek up a dirt trail that paralleled the fire road and plunged down a four foot drop.

"Daredevil David does death defying drops."

"Gotta love those shocks," he said.

We emerged from the trees into a clearing dominated by huge water tanks covered with graffiti. One tank featured a rendition of Fidel Castro. We stopped for a water break. A sign warned us that we were entering the habitat of mountain lions. Mountain lion attacks on humans used to be extremely rare, but as development reduced their habitat and human prey invaded it, they'd become more common, with several attacks in the last few years.

As we ventured into their turf, I persisted, "Is that all? They serve Tang instead of juice?"

"That's pretty criminal when they charge a four thousand dollar deposit and three thousand dollars a month, but no, that's not all," David said indignantly. "There are lots of complaints of understaffing."

"You said that's pretty routine."

"Three weeks ago, one of their dementia patients got loose and went wandering down Capitola Road."

"How did that happen?"

"Someone left a gate unlocked."

It all sounded so mundane. For the family of the Alzheimer's patient, the experience must have been upsetting, but as David explained, the old man had been quickly spotted and returned.

"This all seems like it could happen anywhere," I puffed. It was challenging to keep up with David and to converse at the same time.

"True. Most facilities do have a couple of deficiencies each inspection, but Harbor View Estates has a lot. Would you want your mom there?"

"No. But I don't want my mom in any rest home. What other dirt do you have on this place?"

"Unlocked medical supplies."

"That's serious."

"I've saved the best for last," David gloated. "Which is generally true of me. Which is why you need to stay with me."

"Enough already. Cough it up."

"A suspicious death was attributed to them two months ago.

A Mildred Levine."

"Was it investigated?"

"Not as a criminal matter."

"Why not?"

We emerged from the redwoods into golden foothills. I reached down to the cage for my water bottle and squirted water into my mouth. It tasted like dust.

"First of all, she didn't die at Harbor View. She'd been transferred to a skilled nursing facility. By that time she had a hundred problems—dehydration, over-medication, decubitis . . . ."

"Decubitis?" I pedaled hard to stay at David's side.

"Ulcerated skin. Bed sores. So who would a person prosecute? The minimum wage Mexican girl who didn't turn her enough, who'd probably claim it was the aide on the other shift? Do you go after the nurse?"

He wasn't even breathing hard; it was most annoying.

"The woman Gladys that my mom met seemed to think the nurse was to blame."

"Oh," David said, "you already know about this."

"It was mentioned in passing."

"Do you think the nurse should be locked up for the death?"

I thought of the woman's quick, efficient response to my mom. "She's not even Harbor View Estates' employee," I defended.

"So there you go," he said. "Criminal prosecution would have to go after some eight-dollar-an-hour aide."

"So nothing was done?"

"Leonard issued civil penalties for the decubitis before Mildred was ever transferred. And the family is building a wrongful death case against Harbor View. A civil suit. It'll hit them in the pocketbook. But the family has their work cut out for them. HVE is part of a corporate chain. They have great lawyers."

"I guess they serve Tang so they can afford them."

"You've got it. Anyone who thinks big corporate facilities are in business because they care about old people is living in Ozzie and Harrietville."

That, I thought, *would be my mom.*

We crossed Empire Grade Road into a ranch called Grey Whale. Grey Whale now linked to the coastal Wilder Ranch, a state park. We could ride for miles with vistas of the ocean and detours of single tracks into the woods and across creeks.

Across a field of rattlesnake grass, I heard a short, keening squeal. A death cry. My eyes followed the sound.

I pointed for David. In the distance, under a live oak, I could make out the rounded hairy backs of two wild boars. As they rooted into their prey, they snuffled and grunted in satisfaction.

After watching for a couple of minutes, David mused, "The Levine family has a shot, though. As we are learning from the O.J. trial, civil cases are easier to win than criminal cases. You only need a preponderance of evidence instead of proof beyond reasonable doubt."

We took off and sped up for a downhill stretch. I flew behind David, eating his dust and catching air on the bumps. He waited for me at the bottom where the trail forked.

"How'd you like that?" he grinned.

I skidded to a stop and nodded. "It seems to me like it would be easy to murder someone in a facility."

"You," he said, rapping on my black Giro helmet, "have an evil mind."

CHAPTER 7

I swung my Ghia off Soquel Drive on to Capitola Road. My mom gripped the battered seat. Since I was neither speeding nor careless, this perturbed me. I was cranky anyway from getting up at four a.m. to bake blueberry buckle for the eating elite. I made huge sheets of the stuff, but a normal recipe would be:

2 cups flour
$3/4$ cup sugar
2 $1/2$ teaspoons baking powder
a dash of salt
$1/4$ cup soft butter
$3/4$ cup milk
1 egg
2 cups well-drained blueberries

Heat oven to 375. Grease an 8x8x2 or 9x9x2 pan. Blend all the ingredients except berries. Beat vigorously. Then slowly fold in berries. Spread in pan. Top batter with a mix of $1/2$ cup sugar, $1/3$ cup flour, $1/2$ teaspoon cinnamon and $1/4$ cup soft butter. Bake 45 to 50 minutes.

The Ghia easily took the hairpin turn off Capitola Road to climb the hill to Harbor View Estates. Rusty and ratty as it was, I loved my Poor Man's Porsche. Italian design meets German efficiency. What could be finer?

Before David had entered my life, I would have called Harbor View Estates an old folks' home. Now that I'd been schooled, I knew old folks' home was a lay person's generic term. Residential care facilities, like Harbor View Estates, were basically hotels for old people. They included meals and maid service and offered people various degrees of assistance. The Department of Social Services licensed these businesses. Skilled nursing facilities were an entirely different affair. Skilled nursing facilities were set up to offer medical care and were licensed by the Department of Health.

After I parked, I ran around the Ghia to open the creaky door and to help my mom up from the low seat.

"Good grief, Carol," she said, batting me away. She took a moment to make a bow of the tie on her pink blouse, possibly so people wouldn't notice it was the same blouse she'd worn on her first visit. She fished two big bouquets of sunflowers from the back of the car.

As we made our way down the hall toward 302, Chrissie ran from the room. "Ohmygod, ohmygod, ohmygod. Did you see the nurse?"

"What's the matter?" my mom asked.

I sprinted toward room 302.

"Don't go in there!" Chrissie screamed at me. "I already called 911. Where's the nurse? Did you see her? Ohmygod."

"I'm going to use the emergency call in her room," I shouted over my shoulder.

"No, no, no," the girl said. "Help me find the nurse!" She took off down the hall, but I hustled to the room. The emergency cord was flipped over the shower curtain bar. I pulled it down and yanked it.

My mom entered as I was bending over Gladys. Gladys had kicked back her maroon Lazyboy to a full recline and would have looked asleep except that her green eyes were open and her hands were clutched at her collar. I pulled free a hand and felt for a pulse.

Chrissie returned to the room. "The nurse is coming," she explained. Her voice sounded slurred and her pupils looked constricted.

My mom had dropped the bouquets of sunflowers on the floor and had her ear bent to Gladys's mouth. "Any luck?" she asked me.

I shook my head. I couldn't feel any pulse.

Fire engines in the distance shrilled and honked there way up Soquel Drive. The noise was heavenly. Both the fire department and hospital were within a mile, but the response still seemed amazingly fast. How long ago had the girl called 911?

"Do either of you know how to give CPR?" my mom asked.

"I wasn't scheduled for that training until November," Chrissie said defensively. "Besides Harbor View tells all its staff not to do anything, just call 911."

"Well she really should be flat, but I don't think even the three of us can lift her out of this chair." My mom kicked the sunflowers out of the way, deftly loosened the woman's blouse and tilted back the pale face topped with garish red hair. "Bring me her tank," she commanded Chrissie.

"It's not here."

"Not here?" my mom exclaimed.

"She had a bad week and used up her supply." The girl stood in the kitchen nook and bit at her fingernails.

My mom listened again for any hint of breathing.

"I came back from lunch and she was like this," Chrissie volunteered.

Given Chrissie's condition, her lunch must have featured entrees of Demerol.

My mom ignored Chrissie, and to my astonishment, slipped a small, one way breathing mask from her purse and placed it over Gladys's mouth. She pinched the woman's nose and breathed into her.

I glanced at the clock above the refrigerator. It was 3:33.

Nurse Motha was the first help to arrive at the small apartment.

"Good work," she told my mom.

"She's a dental hygienist," I explained lamely.

"I'll take over," the nurse said, crowding my mom from the body. The nurse did not resume the CPR, but felt for vital signs.

The paramedics and the administrator, Katherine O'Conner, converged on the small apartment at the same time.

Katherine O'Conner herded us into the hallway. A woman who looked like she might come up to about my clavicle emerged from two doors down. "What's happened to Gladys?"

"We don't know yet, Ida," Katherine O'Conner said. "Nurse Motha is with her now."

"Oh, that's comforting."

I never would have expected sarcasm from the lady. She looked prim from her white hair to her tiny, pristine white tennis shoes.

She hobbled toward us, using a black cane for support. "Is she dead?" Ida demanded.

"We'll know about her condition soon," Katherine O'Conner said calmly.

My mom shook her head and said to me in a low voice, "She's deader than a doorknob."

CHAPTER 8

Normally that would have been all she wrote. Harbor View Estates was an anticipated last address. Such facilities kept the client's written wishes on file and the desired funeral home arrived within an hour. The family was called and the body discreetly removed. Unless something aroused the mortician's suspicion, he signed the death certificate.

"A fine death," my mom pronounced.

Gladys had been alert and feisty to the end. She'd died relaxed in her favorite chair gazing out over Arana Gulch. I was inclined to agree with my mom. Short of passing away in one's sleep, I couldn't imagine a more peaceful death. I'd pick it any day to the slow withering away of my brother. Donald had considered himself lucky to be able to tie up all the loose ends and to say goodbye to everyone who mattered. But then Donald not only had hogged the feminine genes and Latino good looks, but also had stolen all the cheerful optimism in the family.

Gladys Mills' end suited my nature; I'd definitely prefer to drop dead on the floor. But when my mom called the funeral home to find out the time of the memorial service, she discovered it had been delayed to allow for an autopsy.

"We have to invite Leonard to dinner," I told David. As the licensing analyst for Harbor View Estates, Leonard might know why an autopsy had been ordered.

"I assume that means you want me to cook," David grumped. We sat on the sunny brick patio outside my sliding glass door.

"Of course." I may have been a spectacular baker at work, but I wasn't a cook.

Lola sprawled on her back in front of us and I obligingly petted her belly. David poked jealously at her dark fur with the toe of his running shoes. It was meant to torment Lola, but she purred. "Lola would be traumatized by a move," I said, continuing The Battle of the Abode.

David ignored the comment. "I'm not inviting the whole family." He meant Leonard Glass's family. Although David had managed to raise a son of his own, he did not like children. After years of struggling as a single father, he'd had his fill. "Babies are like gas," he quipped. "You can only stand the smell of your own."

"Of course not. Only Leonard." I twisted around and peered into my house. "I love wood floors. That's why Chad and I bought this house."

"I like carpet," David said with finality. "What can I say to Noreen?" David also did not like Leonard's wife.

"Tell her you want to borrow Leonard for a photo shoot."

He grinned, a big smile full of straight white teeth, one of the first features I'd loved about David. In addition to his job as an investigator, David earned money by taking nudey pictures for skin magazines.

"I'll tell Leonard that you're going to be in the pictures with him. Let him figure out what to tell Noreen."

"That should work." According to Leonard, I was his dream goddess. He wanted to be the first to know should David have a terminal illness.

Leonard was a tall man with ropy muscles from biking, surfing and chasing children. His silver hair reached his shoulders and contrasted with his smooth skin to make him appear more youthful than his forty-five years.

He gave me a sideways hug and a kiss on the cheek and

handed David a bottle of wine. He sniffed the air. "Ah, let me guess." He closed his eyes like a psychic connecting with spirit guides and his long fingers formed mudras. "Pampano en papillote?" He sniffed some more. "Or maybe coquilles St. Jacques?"

He knew damn well we were having spaghetti. It was the only dish David served.

"What did you tell Noreen?" David asked.

"I told her I was coming here."

Noreen was a stay-at-home mom who doted on her four children. David barely tolerated children, even good-looking, intelligent, well-behaved ones like Leonard and Noreen's. But even if David had adored children, Noreen didn't want her fourteen, eleven, nine and six year old around a devil incarnate who played blaring rap music and took pictures of naked women. Especially on a school night.

"If I'm not home by nine, Noreen will call the cops," Leonard said.

"I'll cook the noodles."

"That would be a lot faster on my gas range," I said.

We moved into the kitchen and popped the cork on the wine, a much finer cabernet than David or I ever bought. "I have so much to tell you guys," Leonard said, lounging on a stool at the butcher block table.

"You have to admit this kitchen is great," David retaliated, "and you can change a stove a lot easier than a floor plan."

Even with brown linoleum and harvest gold appliances, David's country kitchen was wonderful, with lots of room and big windows looking into the back yard.

Leonard's eyes bounced between us. "Am I interrupting something here?"

"Besides the World Federation Wrestling Smack Down Carol and I were having when you rang the bell?"

"What a coincidence. Noreen and I have our competitions

on Tuesday, too."

"So what do you have to tell us?" I asked.

Leonard stroked his silver hair and tucked it behind his ear. "First of all, the son, Rusty Mills has made a complaint against Harbor View alleging abuse and neglect. With this Gladys Mills thing on top of the Mildred Levine case, I'll be inspecting Harbor View Estates weekly," Leonard announced. "Depending on what we turn up, you could be called in David."

"Why's that?"

"Well you know the son demanded an autopsy?"

David poured the spaghetti noodles into a colander, rinsed them with hot water and shook them vigorously. I took down three plates from the cupboard and we served ourselves buffet style. The green salad and garlic bread were already on the dining room table.

"So what did the autopsy show?" I asked as we settled at the pine table.

"Gladys Mills had recently received an injection. Intramuscular. The needle prick would have been overlooked except there was erythema around it."

"She was murdered?" If my mouth hadn't been stuffed with spaghetti, I would have been shouting.

"Whoa, whoa, whoa," Leonard said. "No one's jumping to the M word."

"What's erythema?" David asked.

"It just means redness," Leonard said.

Topping off his wine, David asked seriously, "Did Gladys take injected medication?"

"Nah. Not that the facility has on record. But she might have been given someone else's shot."

"You mean the nurse accidentally gave Gladys Mills an injection," I said incredulously, "instead of, say, the woman in 301?"

"Exactly," Leonard replied as he fished curls of carrot out of his salad. "That kind of thing happens more than people would want to know."

"Jesus. Remind me never to get old." Still, old and ill as she may have been, I couldn't imagine a spirited woman like Gladys Mills sedately accepting an unexpected needle, especially from a nurse she didn't like. When my mom and I and Chrissie had seen the body, there had been no evidence of a struggle. "What if the injection weren't an accident?"

Leonard laughed. "David's right about you. You do have an evil mind."

My face burned. I was used to the outside world thinking I was weird, but I expected more respect from two people who routinely investigated.

"It's quite possible the shot was not an accident," Leonard said in a conciliatory tone. "But that doesn't mean murder. Assisted living residents aren't prisoners. They only receive help with their medication if they need it. Gladys could have been to a doctor or given herself an injection or even had someone she trusted give her an injection. Her private life is not the facility's business."

Of course Leonard was right. Gladys's personal assistant and rebellious smoking showed she was the type to have arranged shots without Harbor View Estates' knowledge. But with twenty-twenty hindsight, there had been suspicious elements to Gladys's death, such as the emergency cord flipped over the shower stall, easy enough for an able-bodied, five-foot-eight person like me to reach, but another matter for a much shorter woman who had difficulty using a walker.

On the other hand, it didn't look like Gladys had even attempted to get out of her chair. Her hands had looked as though she'd meant to rip open her collar, as though she'd had trouble breathing, a perfectly logical end for a woman with some sort of bronchial ailment.

"Well what did the autopsy show she'd been injected with?"

I asked, still miffed.

"Come on, Carol," Leonard said, shoving back his silver hair. "I just meant that it's not usual to meet a woman who thinks like you."

I stabbed a cherry tomato and produced a satisfying spurt. "So what did the autopsy show?" I prodded more calmly. I abandoned the tomato and took a bite of spaghetti, but it no longer tasted good.

"Unknown at this point."

"Why did this Rusty Mills guy want an autopsy in the first place?" David asked. He'd been unusually quiet.

"I don't know. I heard a rumor that the will wasn't what he expected."

"So he thinks it was foul play, too," I crowed.

"Foul play," Leonard said. He laid down his fork so that he could concentrate all his energy on laughing at me.

CHAPTER 9

If I'd stopped to think about other people, I never would have stuck my nose into this case. But with my usual stubbornness and self-absorption, I found myself, the next afternoon, on the way to visit Gladys's son, Rusty a.k.a. Russell Mills. Since I'd been logging hours with David's friend, J.J. Sloan, bona fide PI, I had some shaky authority on which to base my snooping.

I hadn't told David about my plans. I hadn't made any plans. I'd finished baking for the day, called Mills' Construction on Freedom Boulevard, and a secretary had informed me that if I wanted to talk to Rusty in person, I'd find him on site, a small housing development off Chanticleer.

Chanticleer ran through the heart of Live Oak, David's neighborhood. The unincorporated area was being transformed into a bedroom community for Silicon Valley commuters. Run down houses on acre plots were being leveled and replaced with cul-de-sacs of soulless two-story monster homes.

A power line angled down from the nearest pole to Rusty Mill's small blue and white trailer at the front of a development in progress. I climbed the cinder block steps and entered a dingy, hot room just large enough to serve as an office. The thin carpet was tracked with dirt and Rusty Mills sat behind a battered desk with a heap of papers shoved to one side. He boomed into a cellular phone, eyed me quizzically, and waved for me to sit in one of the two folding metal chairs in front of his desk. A dusty fan riffled a calendar hanging on the thin paneling, but Rusty's graying hair was still damp with sweat.

Rusty turned off the phone. He was a handsome, big-chested man of about fifty with gray-green eyes. "How may I help you?" He pulled a full ashtray in front of him, but hesitated to light up.

Like mother, like son, I thought. Nothing predisposed a person to smoke like having a chimney for a mom. I explained that my mom and I had known his mother and expressed sympathy for his loss.

"I appreciate that." He tapped a cigarette on the desk.

"I don't mind if you smoke." In truth, I'd rather scrub a toilet with a toothbrush, but Rusty Mills would be much more cooperative if he had the cigarette he craved. And he already seemed to be wondering why I hadn't just sent a sympathy card.

"My mom called the funeral home to find out the time of the service but was told that they didn't know when it would be because of the autopsy."

He lit a Marlboro. In blue jeans and tee-shirt, he could have been Marlboro's billboard ad. In addition to the calendar, the wall supported an American flag and a small framed photo.

He squinted at me from behind the smoke and remained silent. He wiped his forehead with the back of his hand. He rolled back in his desk chair as if to get a better look at me. Unlike his mom, he didn't seem eager to talk.

"So we wondered what happened to your mom?"

Outside the fan's arc, I sat in the hot box, perspired, and waited for his answer. I concentrated on trying to make out what was in the framed picture. I resisted the temptation to fill his silence.

"Mom died, but the circumstances didn't seem right," he finally said.

"What seemed wrong?"

Rusty smoked and regarded me. I prided myself on my

ability at stare-downs. I'd once defeated my brother Donald after twenty-two minutes. But Rusty Mills was making me nervous.

"How do you feel about environmental activists?" he asked.

"What?"

"You know, groups like Earth Love. What do you think of them?"

Given that Rusty Mills was in construction, I sensed what the "right" answer might be. "They're a little radical."

The muddy green eyes didn't change. Under the whir of the fan, the pop of a nail gun and the muffled shouts of men permeated the trailer.

"A little," Rusty said dryly. "Do you have a badge or something like that?"

I handed him my card from Sloan's.

"A private investigator?" He smoked thoughtfully for a few seconds. "Did Melanie hire you?" he asked deprecatingly.

"Your ex-wife?" I said to let him know I knew a thing or two. "No."

"Who do you represent?"

"I thought you might like to hire me."

"What are you? Some sort of ambulance chaser?" He leaned back, propped steel-toed construction boots on the desk, and inspected me. "The State has people to look into my mom's treatment at Harbor View."

I felt an incipient moral dilemma. If I really wanted this man to hire me, I should disparage the State's investigation. I should discredit David's office and Leonard's competence. Certainly nobody at Community Care Licensing would be volunteering information to Rusty about Mildred Levine. And that case could add substance if Rusty decided to follow up his complaint with a civil suit.

I had a plethora of information about Harbor View that the State might not volunteer, such as the understaffing and unlocked meds. Even though complaints were a matter of public record, and Rusty's lawyers could dredge them up, they'd charge a lot more than Sloan's Investigative Services.

I should have been saying this to Rusty, selling myself. Instead I stayed quiet. All of my information had been shared with me in confidence.

Rusty Mills asked, "Are these State investigators any good or are they just paper-shuffling bureaucrats?"

I hesitated. In that pause was betrayal. "I think they'll do a fine job." If Rusty Mills was contemplating a civil suit against Harbor View Estates, a lot of cash could hang in the balance of the investigation.

My hesitation was meant to leave doubt in Rusty Mills' mind.

"When was the last time you saw your mom?" I inquired, expecting Rusty Mills to indicate it was time for me to leave.

"The day she died." He reached forward to stub out his cigarette, but stayed in his contemplative, leaned back posture. He reminded me of his mom in her Lazyboy. He laced his fingers behind his head. He rolled his head and his neck cracked and popped. "I tell you what," he said. "I think you're a ballsy gal. If I had the money, I'd hire you. There are things I'd like to find out about."

Like why your mom changed her will, I thought.

"We offer a great service at a great price." I sounded like Wendy Keegan, the sales associate at Harbor View Estates.

"Thanks for your card," Rusty Mills said. He swung his legs off the desk and stood to shake my hand.

CHAPTER 10

J.J. Sloan's office was in a building across from the courthouse. The depressing rectangle of gray stucco also housed the legal aide who'd helped me with the paperwork on my divorce.

If you blinked, you'd miss the narrow passage to parking in the back. There were moments, like now, when I wondered how I could possibly prefer this world to that of my baking job at Archibald's with its surrounding forest, green manicured lawns, and lush flower beds. This was a utilitarian, destination stop with a single-width door. The hall was narrow and dim and opened into small, cramped offices. Ours was the second on the right. It was locked. I didn't bother to stop to see if I had messages. Instead I headed to J.J. Sloan's real office, the bar up the street.

J.J. Sloan was a caricature of a person he'd never become, someone like Hemingway at the end of his life if he'd only been a writer rather than a famous author.

J.J. took his drinking seriously and regarded people who couldn't keep up as wimps; since he managed to function in life, it never crossed his mind that he was an alcoholic. Fortunately, because I was a woman, I wasn't expected to keep up.

The day he'd hired me, he'd taken me to this very bar for celebratory drinks. It met his requirements of being open early and pouring a solid drink at a fair price. Inside it was dusky and smelly with decrepit human fixtures on the stools. To J.J. these were the real people, unlike the phonies of corporate America, the corrupt successful, the middle class mental midgets, and liberal idiots. If I'd tried to keep up with J.J., I would have been dead from alcohol poisoning my first day on the job.

He'd started with a double margarita which he'd pushed toward the bartender for a little extra on the top.

"I'll take a floater, too," I'd boldly said.

"That's a float, Carol." J.J. had scrunched his pock-marked face into a smile. "Floaters are dead bodies you find in the water."

He talked to me like I was an imbecile most of the time.

It was because of J.J. that I now owned a gun and a permit to carry a concealed weapon. I'd purchased the same type of revolver David owned, a thirty-eight caliber Colt Detective Special.

It didn't live up to J.J.'s standard of sexiness, but it was gloriously simple and reliable.

Today I found him on his stool at the end of the bar. He was dressed in his usual jeans and sneakers. He had to be prepared to "catch a case." He used what he imagined to be hip street lingo. It seemed affected, but was completely ingrained.

Even though his name suggested an East Coast retailer of yuppie clothes, J.J. Sloan's mother was Jewish and he was from Detroit where he and David Shapiro had met thirty years ago in Hebrew School. Their childhood friendship, their loyalty to the Red Wings hockey team, and their shared interest in investigation were the ties that continued their bond.

"Yo," he addressed me, patting the stool beside him. J.J. looked like a former hockey player with his smashed nose and capped front teeth. He was drinking a Guinness, but God only knew which number it was.

Unlike most bars, this one had a clock off to the side; its patrons were not the type to be disturbed by the time. J.J. caught me glancing at it. He pushed back his lank blond hair and grinned with his oversized teeth. "Follow the rules of Zen, Carol. When you are hungry, eat. When you are thirsty, drink. When you are tired, sleep."

I wasn't thirsty, but I ordered a Red Tail anyway to be sociable and told J.J. about the death of Gladys Mills and my visit to her son's construction site.

"Well, if this fish bites," J.J. said, "you take the case."

If Rusty Mills decided to employ Sloan's Investigative Services, there wasn't anything about his mother's death that was racy enough for J.J. Sloan, even if it had been murder.

J.J. yawned and tapped his finger on the bar to indicate to the bartender he wanted another Guinness. "I've got me a tasty combo platter," he said. "A little robbery and sodomy with a minor." He purposely withheld the details, underscoring that while he trusted my competence enough to give me carte blanche with Rusty Mills, he still regarded me as a civilian. That's what J.J. Sloan called all people not linked to the world of street crime, all people offended by his humor or anyone who looked askance at his wake-up bloody Mary with a float on top.

CHAPTER 11

The fact I didn't have a client had never stopped me from snooping in the past and I didn't see any reason to let it stop me now. After my beer with J.J., I headed to Harbor View Estates.

There were many ways into the facility that skirted the reception area, but I didn't believe an outsider had wandered into the facility and killed Gladys Mills. Nor did I believe her death was an accident.

I padded down the wing with Gladys Mills' room and stopped at 306. I believed Gladys Mills' death had been murder, and like most murders, it had been personal. If I wanted to find the killer, I needed to know more about Gladys Mills.

Nearly every resident had something on his or her door to individualize it. Ida Walker's door was adorned with a wrought iron welcome sign graced with hummingbirds. I rapped, but no one answered. I tried several more times, thinking that an old woman might be hard of hearing or might need a lot of time to make it to the door.

Then I remembered where I was. It was about five thirty; the clients were eating. I headed for the dining hall and found Ida with a woman and a man at a table for four. Ida and the man were silently poking at cups of fruit salad, but the other woman was feasting on a large bowl of vanilla ice cream drenched in caramel syrup.

"I remember you," Ida Walker said brightly. Today she wore a blue pantsuit with flowers appliquéd across the chest and stylish blue plastic earrings with gold trim. I remembered Gladys saying Ida Walker had picked fruit during The Thirties. She was so tiny I wondered how she could have reached anything.

"This is Jack Dorfman."

The butt grabber with all his marbles, I recalled.

The tall, craggy man inspected me up and down and nodded his head as though I were an animal at auction and he was considering a bid. He had a big nose and a fringe of gray around an age spotted pate.

"And this is Harriet McGruder." Harriet had a walker parked by her chair and Jack and Ida had canes hanging from the backs of their seats. "Are you going to work here?" Harriet asked.

"Not in a matter of speaking," I said.

Harriet returned to industriously eating ice cream.

"That chair," Ida nodded somberly toward the vacant seat, "belonged to Gladys."

The three mournfully considered the vacant spot and I felt relieved that I hadn't presumed to sit, defiling the temple.

"And who is this lovely gal?" Jack gruffly demanded of Ida. "You haven't introduced her."

Ida's sweet blue eyes rolled up to me. She blushed, struggling to recall my name.

"Carol Sabala," I said. "I don't think we were ever introduced, Ida."

Jack Dorfman shakily raised himself onto his cane and held out his large, knobby hand. As I shook it, his cane dropped to the carpet and he grabbed my hip to steady himself. His hand slid down and he gave my butt a firm squeeze. "Excuse me," he said. "I'm not usually so clumsy."

"Like hell," Ida scolded. "Sit down, Jack, and behave yourself."

Jack obeyed, with a complacent smile on his wrinkled face.

A teenage waitress came by and picked up Jack's cane. "Up to your old tricks, Jack?" Unlike Chrissie, this girl looked wholesome.

"Will you be joining the group for the meal?" she asked me.

In Jack's company, it might be a good idea to get seated.

"Take a load off," Jack said.

"Is it okay if I sit here?" I motioned to the empty seat. I didn't consider myself very superstitious, but the idea of taking a dead woman's spot felt creepy. "I'm going to pass on dinner, though."

Ida waved me into the seat.

"Are you going to work here?" Harriet asked me again.

I shook my head.

"Carol and her mom found Gladys," Ida explained to the other woman. "Harriet has all her marbles," Ida whispered apologetically, "it's just some days she can't remember where she put them."

"I wanted to talk to you about Gladys," I said to the group.

They all dejectedly looked at the chair and seemed surprised to find me in it.

"Gladys," Jack pronounced. "She had a great, big, plump . . . ." He paused dramatically. "Heart." He sniggered.

Ida rolled her eyes and sighed. "Let's talk in my room, honey."

"What? You're going to take the party and run away?" Jack asked.

Ida lifted herself carefully on to her black cane. "How could that be, Jack? You're the party, aren't you?"

She hobbled toward her room and I followed. "What did you want to know about Gladys, honey?"

Before I could answer, she said, "You know Gladys and I first met at the end of The Depression. We've known each other nigh on sixty years."

"This must be a very sad time for you."

She bobbed her head. "Yes." Her thoughts drifted away. I felt like slinging her over my shoulders like a sack of potatoes so we could move a little faster.

Other old people were shuffling down the hallway, most of them with walkers or canes. I sensed they could move faster, but when your life was reduced to egg salad sandwiches for lunch, conversations with half-lucid companions, and television, what was the big hurry? Since this was a likely destination for many of us, why did any of us rush?

Ida's apartment was a duplicate of Gladys's. She even had a similarly positioned Lazyboy, albeit ivory-colored and smaller. She settled herself into her chair. I sat on the matching couch.

The old lady gazed out her window and didn't say anything.

I began to wish we'd stayed at the table. While Ida was lucid, she seemed to lose her train of thought. I didn't relish intruding on her grief.

"Did Gladys seem all right to you the day she passed away?" I asked softly.

Ida turned to me with a small, ironic smile. "Oh sure. She just had her usual wheezing and hacking and suicidal cigarette smoking on top of her chronic bronchitis."

"So you're not surprised that she died?"

"It's a shock, but not a surprise."

"Gladys didn't have any oxygen in her room that day."

"That's not unusual," Ida said. "She wasn't dependent on her tank, so if it needed a refill, it didn't necessarily get replaced immediately. Since this place is always short-staffed, non-emergencies have a low priority."

"Who was responsible for checking on her tanks?"

"Rusty paid the nurse to keep an eye on them."

"I thought people didn't like Nurse Motha."

"She's what's available."

"Was Gladys receiving any injections?"

"Not that I know of, and I knew her pretty well." The woman reached into a capacious bag beside her chair and fished out knitting needles stuck into a half-finished, tiny white sweater. She rested the materials in her lap. "Why do you ask?"

"The autopsy revealed a needle prick."

Ida blanched. "Is that so?" She studied the tiny white garment in her lap as though it had landed from outer space.

"For a grandchild?" I asked.

She shook her head. "My Will and I, we never bothered with kids."

I didn't know whether I'd committed one of my frequent faux pas or whether the woman, like myself, had chosen a child-free life.

"I look at Gladys and her Rusty and I think it's just as well." She raised the needles and her withered hands set off as though they had a mind of their own. "One of the kitchen staff is expecting a baby."

"Didn't Gladys get along with her son?"

Ida's hands stopped. "I've always felt sorry for Rusty. Being an only child, everything was expected of him. He tried to serve as Gladys's father, husband, handyman, nurse, and confidant."

"And Gladys was a demanding person."

"Oh, boy," Ida said. She plucked up her knitting only to throw it down in her lap. "That woman was more demanding than Moses with his ten commandments."

"Oh," she said again, and without any other sound or warning, tears began running down her face.

The tissue box was next to her on a coffee table so I sat ineffectually on the couch to wait out the spate of grief. I knew only too well, from my brother Donald's death, how grief could pounce, sudden and unexpected, and rip into your heart.

Ida dried her tears. "Here I am, talking ill of the dead. Some friend I am."

"Love isn't blind," I said. "Love is seeing someone the way he, or she, is and loving the person anyway."

"That's sweet," Ida said.

It did sound lovely, but in my relationship with David

Shapiro, selective blindness could serve us both.

"Would you like a glass of water?"

"Yes. Thank you."

The sandy-colored Formica was immaculate. I wondered if any of the residents ate in their apartments when they could receive a meal in the dining room, the hub of social activity. I found glasses in the logical cupboard, brought Ida water, and resettled on the couch.

"Do you think Rusty loved his mother?" I asked bluntly.

"Rusty was a good kid," Ida replied, sipping the water. "I've known him all his life and he's always been a responsible boy. Dedicated to his mom."

Cherish, appreciate, prize, adore, idolize, treasure. A thesaurus would list a lot of synonyms for love. I wondered if responsibility and dedication would be among them.

"What about Rusty's dad?"

Ida sighed deeply. "He was a lovely man. He started Mills' Construction."

"What happened to him?" Even to myself, I sounded too direct. I really needed to work on my people skills.

Ida sat aside the water. "A terrible accident."

She pulled around the little garment and positioned her needles as though she meant to resume knitting, but she didn't. "They'd just started using those nail guns to build houses."

I cringed at what was coming.

"One of his young workers shot him in the temple." She raised one of her small, delicate hands to the side of her head. "It was awful."

Ida's hand returned to her lap and she sat, stunned, lost in the memory.

Silence gathered around us. Outside, a chipmunk chirped like a bird. A plane flew overhead.

After a solid two minutes, the woman began to knit.

"I heard a rumor," I said salaciously.

The words had the desired effect. Ida turned toward me, her blue eyes wide, the chrysalis of a smile on her face.

"I heard Gladys changed her will."

"And cut Rusty out?" Ida guessed.

"I don't know."

My news had not given her a gram of glee. She solemnly contemplated the baby sweater as her hands continued their rhythmic dance. "That sounds like Gladys. She liked to flex her muscle."

"Was she mad at Rusty?"

"She was always getting mad at Rusty, and then buying him extravagant toys to make up. They did not have a healthy relationship. They were way too involved in each other's lives."

"Do you know why she was mad at him?"

"I wouldn't know where to start. She was mad at him for not being a daughter. She was mad because he got divorced, even though it wasn't his idea. She felt he should have been doing better with the family business. But she was especially mad when he didn't want to let her live with him. When he put her here, instead."

"How did Rusty deal with all that?"

"He was always a good son."

Surely after fifty years of putting up with Gladys's crap, Rusty Mills had some pent up rage. Gladys sounded like she could inspire fantasies of matricide.

After a quick rap on the door, Nurse Motha stuck her head around the door. "Ida, are you ready for your shot?"

CHAPTER 12

"Tell me, Carol, exactly what you're trying to do?"

David was not happy. He'd come to my place which normally he avoided in order to demonstrate how much he didn't want to live in it. His jaw was clenched and he refused to sit.

I sat at my oak table and leaned back in a chair with my hands clasped behind my thick head of hair. The picture of nonchalance. I reminded myself to breathe. "I'm just snooping around a bit, basically acting like myself."

"Leonard is the licensing agent, Carol."

"I know that." David was dressed for work in his good Levi's and a white shirt and he looked entirely too sexy for an argument.

"Then why are you interfering?" he asked.

"What are you so upset about? Aren't you and Leonard the guys who have the mantra that work is overrated and that careers are for sissies?"

"That doesn't mean we want to lose our jobs." He planted himself in the middle of the room that was my living room, kitchen and eating area combined. "Work as little as possible. That is my motto. If I get fired and can't collect my pension," he explained, "I'll have to work *more*. That goes against all my principles."

I smiled at his self-deprecating irony. It took the edge off the confrontation. I placed my hands on the table and sighed. "I don't understand how my actions undermine Leonard's investigation or how they could get you in trouble."

"Our supervisor would not appreciate learning that my girlfriend, as some kind of hobby, has been interviewing residents about Gladys's death."

"First of all, how would your supervisor know? Secondly, my mom is considering Harbor View Estates as a place to live. Surely I can go there and ask questions. Besides, I know Ida Walker. Can't a private citizen talk to her?"

"Let's take these points one at a time." He ticked off the first point on his pinky. "Our supervisor is visiting Harbor View Estates, too. She would recognize you from the shrine I've erected over my office desk." He moved to the table, sat across from me, and pinned me with his dark eyes. His right index finger slapped the next finger of his left hand. "Secondly, you can talk to Ida Walker, but that's a little different than pumping her for information. By the time Leonard questioned her this afternoon, she wanted to know if you were part of Community Care Licensing."

David's anger was dissipating and I couldn't prevent a small smile. "Ida's pretty sharp."

"That's the problem. When Leonard spoke to her, she acted like she should call a lawyer."

I ran my hands over my oak table. The wood felt alive with memories of my grandmother and the regal tree it had been before that. "I love this table," I announced.

"I think it'll fit in the dining room," he countered.

"It fits better here."

He didn't respond and silence grew between us. His eyes jumped around the room. "This place is too small."

I sensed he felt confined by more than lack of space. He wasn't in charge here. He was a guy who felt relaxed on his home turf. There was no television here. No stereo!

"What if I get hired to investigate?"

"Who would hire you?"

I recoiled as though I'd been slapped.

"I didn't mean it like that. I meant who would your client be?" A warm, confident hand latched on to mine. "Lots of people would hire you. I would hire you."

"Did Leonard find out Ida Walker receives shots?" I asked.

"Yeah. But it's just vitamin B." He released my hand. "Even if the nurse accidentally injected Gladys Mills with Ida's dose of vitamin B, which, of course, the nurse vehemently denies, a megadose of vitamin B wouldn't kill anyone."

"But maybe the nurse gave Gladys someone else's injection."

He shook his head. "Not likely. The way you've described this Gladys, even if the nurse accidentally entered the wrong room, she wouldn't mistake her for some other little old lady.

"According to Leonard," he continued, "even if Harbor View has its problems, the VNA keeps good records. He'll probably visit their office to double check on this nurse, but for right now, she seems okay."

"If there's a logical reason for everything, why was your supervisor at Harbor View?"

"Because the relationship between Harbor View and our office is adversarial. When Leonard cites them, they refuse to post their deficiencies. They appeal every civil penalty. With the Mildred Levine case, they even tried to discredit Leonard by claiming that he's not impartial. He and Noreen are active in Temple Beth El and Mildred Levine's family is a huge donor. So now our supervisor wants two people on every visit so they can't claim Leonard is biased."

"The girl there, Chrissie, told me that Harbor View instructs its employees not to administer first aid, to call 911 instead."

David shrugged. "Par for the course."

"But I got the impression employees are required to have first aid and CPR training."

"It's the law that they have it, not that they use it."

"That's absurd."

"Lawsuits, Carol. The facilities don't want to be liable for employees who bungle the first aid. Even if the staff does everything perfectly, the client still might claim they were too slow or too rough or . . . ." He heaved a sigh at the endless possibilities. "Or something."

Reality was insane. But I could see how the situation had come to be. All I had to do was look at the reputation of Nurse Motha. As the one person at Harbor View who did provide medical care, she struck me as efficient and competent. Yet the residents seemed to regard her as a sadist. It was a wonder they could find anyone to provide medical services.

"Better to call 911," David concluded. "Such is the world we live in."

The scent of honeysuckle wafted through the open window. Years ago, I'd planted a one quart pot on either side, and now the vine circled the window.

"As much as we'd like to nail these fucks, Rusty Mills' charge will probably be unsubstantiated. Even if we knew Gladys Mills had been murdered through some type of lethal injection, it wouldn't necessarily incriminate Harbor View. These are not locked facilities. Anybody could have entered Gladys Mills' room."

"Have you told this to Rusty Mills?"

"According to Leonard, he's been hounding the office, so I'm sure he knows."

Yes! I thought. The more discouraging the report from the state, the more likely I was to hear from Rusty Mills.

David's eyes narrowed. "Please do not tell me he's your potential client."

CHAPTER 13

The call from Rusty Mills was disappointing. He didn't want me to investigate his mother's death. "The State is looking into that," he said glumly. "Of course, if you stumble across any garbage that might advance my civil suit, I'd like to know."

I bit back spilling what Leonard and David had confided in me about Harbor View Estates. If I were going to betray them, I'd want Rusty Mills to pay for it and to think the information had been gathered through my brilliant detection. I did have a couple of tidbits of my own, though. "Did you know your mom was without an oxygen tank the day she died?"

There was a long pause. "That's interesting."

"I'm sure I could find out a whole lot more," I said cockily, "that might advance a wrongful death claim."

He cleared his throat. "I want you to investigate my mom's will."

"I want your best rate," Rusty continued. "Do you have a discount for middle-aged homeowners?"

I appreciated his humor, especially since investigating a will was as exciting as watching Mr. Frederick's neighbor. I had gotten myself into this mess, so I set up a meeting at his trailer for the next afternoon.

Autumn offered Santa Cruz's best weather and the following day was glorious, pushing eighty with not a cloud in sight.

I pulled my trusty Ghia into the construction site. I should have been excited about bringing in my first client; instead I wished that I were riding my bike around the harbor with David. When I spotted Rusty Mills walking toward the office, I jumped from my fully oxidized ride and trotted toward him. The more time we could spend outside his stuffy trailer, the happier I'd be.

Rusty smiled briefly and stuck out his hand. "We meet again, Miss Sabala."

"What a beautiful day," I commented, shaking his hand. He had a powerful grip.

When he released my hand, he dipped into his construction apron, pulled out a small bottle of Maalox, and took a couple of hefty swigs.

He turned toward his development with the pride of a father. To me he could have been gesturing toward Mongoloid Siamese twins joined at the forehead. It was hard to look at. Seven two-story frames on a cul-de-sac crowded what had once been a pastoral plot occupied by a single, run-down bungalow. People were going to be asked to shell out $400,000 for a view out the window of a neighbor's siding.

"Quite an upgrade to the neighborhood," he said.

"I'm sure it will raise property values," I admitted blandly.

People bitched about the increase in traffic in Santa Cruz County. No good plans existed to address the problem. Yet, in spite of the two-lane, country type roads in Live Oak, no housing development seemed to be turned down. An unincorporated area with little political clout, Live Oak was one of the few places in the county with room for expansion. So what if this new development would dump fourteen more automobiles on to the overcrowded streets.

"Let me show you." Rusty sounded like a little boy with a new Tonka truck. He strode down the already paved cul-de-sac to the first unit. We walked up freshly poured concrete with top soil heaped to either side. This unit had most of its plywood walls affixed. He steered me through the door. Bare stairs rose from the left of the foyer. We stepped down to the right, through a kitchen area. Rusty opened a door. In the double garage, a compressor for a nail gun kicked in, forcing Rusty to shout, "That will be a storage attic!"

A construction worker waved down to us. Lines of nails for his gun coiled on the concrete floor like machine gun rounds.

Rusty conducted a full tour of the four bedroom, three bath frame, a monster home cut into awkward cubicles.

I tried to find something to like and ended up complimenting the laundry room and the view of the mountains from the master bedroom.

We walked back toward the trailer. "Can you believe some people thinks it's their right to take a man's hard work and private property and burn it to the ground?"

While I might have liked to burn the place myself, I did take exception to the destruction of another person's property. "Earth Love?" I asked.

"Earth Love," he scoffed. "Criminals. That's what they are."

"They burned down one of your developments?"

"Not that we could prove." He scowled. "But they did." He climbed the two cinder blocks and opened the door to his trailer. I followed him up and into the stink of cigarettes. The trailer was as hot as a tin can that had been cooking in the sun. I'd picked myself the client from hell.

Rusty flopped into his desk chair, switched on the fan, and took another glug of Maalox. This seemed to mark the start of business, but my eye was caught by the fluttering calendar and the single photo.

"Is that you?" I pointed at the photo.

Rusty reached around, unhooked it from the wall and handed it across the desk. It was a yellow newspaper photograph showing a young soldier receiving a handshake from an officer.

"That's me, receiving my purple heart and bronze star."

"Vietnam?" I guessed. He looked the right age, fiftyish.

He nodded his head. "Medic."

"Are you a doctor?"

He chuckled. "Hardly. I was in college, studying biology at the time. I guess the army decided that qualified me to train as a medic."

"Purple heart," I murmured. "That means you were wounded."

He pulled down the neck of his tee-shirt and hunched up his left shoulder to show me the scar. "We were so desperate for medics that they would have kept me there except I'm left handed."

Even though Rusty's tone was light, his face was grim, his eyes vacant, looking back.

"Did you enlist?" I asked. The average soldiers in Vietnam were not college students from well-off families; college students had deferments and lawyers.

He nodded and gave the faintest hint of a smile. "Yup. It sure killed my love of biology." He tapped the glass over the yellowed newspaper photo. "Congressional Medal of Honor, Gold Star, Silver Star and then Bronze Star. Fourth highest medal in the United States.

"I take this with me," he explained, "so every day I can count my luck that I came home with two medals instead of all fucked up or in a coffin." He returned the framed photo to the spot on the cheap paneling. "When I joined the army is just one of many times my mom made it clear I was to be her heir. Even though she was a red-blooded, God-fearing American who supported the war, she was so upset, me being her only child, what if I were killed, who would carry on, and all that shit."

I sat in the hard folding chair across from Rusty. The breeze from the fan ruffled his salt and pepper hair but did nothing for me.

"I've seen her wills over the years," he continued, "and I've always been listed as the primary beneficiary."

"When did you find out you weren't?"

"The day she died."

You certainly didn't waste any time, I thought.

As though sensing my thoughts, Rusty said, "Her will contained specific directions for the funeral arrangements. I needed to refresh my memory, so I went to the lawyer's office. I'm still listed as the executor and the lawyer's an old family friend. He let me see the whole thing."

"So to whom did she leave the estate?"

"She left a lot of the property to Planned Parenthood."

Ouch! I thought. *How should one's offspring interpret that?*

"She also left the family house to Chrissie. Nothing fancy, but on West Cliff with an ocean view. In Santa Cruz's market, it should be worth over a mil."

Now this was getting interesting. Chrissie had all the symptoms of a drug user. Pills were my guess. *A pill popper might do a lot to get her hands on a million dollars.*

Rusty laced his hands behind his head and leaned back. "She left some money to Melanie and the kids, a bunch of sentimental stuff to Ida, and fifty thousand to me."

"So she didn't cut you out completely."

Rusty shrugged and sighed. "She may as well have. Fifty thousand doesn't make any difference in my life. It certainly won't take care of the financing on this project."

Working with Rusty was going to be like baking pastries. I didn't like sweets much, but I still did a good job with them. Rusty was so different from me—a smoker who could dismiss fifty thousand dollars. With fifty thousand, I could take two years off my baking job.

"So what is it you want me to find out?" I asked. "You don't suspect forgery, do you?"

Rusty leaned forward and crossed muscular arms over his

thick chest. "I'm not one hundred percent convinced this is the real deal. I considered having it examined by a documents expert at the San Francisco Crime Lab. I've heard of people doing things like keeping the signature page, but changing all the other information. Up there at the lab, they have equipment that can tell if one ink is different from another. But then I asked myself, "Who would forge a will and leave property to Planned Parenthood?'"

Someone who hates you. However, since even Rusty thought the will was written by his dear, departed mother, I kept this idea to myself.

"I plan to contest this will," Rusty explained. "I want you to dig up evidence of an unsound mind or undue influence."

I sat silently for a moment, feeling the sweat pop out of my forearms and behind my ears. Was Rusty suggesting I fabricate evidence? Gladys had certainly seemed of sound mind to me. And who would have wanted to coerce Gladys to leave her money to Planned Parenthood?

"I should talk to Chrissie," I said. I relished talking to the girl. Gladys's personal assistant should know a lot about the woman's mental health, provided Chrissie wasn't too high to notice. Besides, the girl had a million dollar motive for murder. While on behalf of my client, I was legitimately chatting to Chrissie about Gladys's moods, I might work the conversation around to mysterious injections and a missing oxygen tank.

"That would be a good start," Rusty said. He scribbled on a paper. "I want a full report. Everything you learn about this girl." He handed me an address and phone number. "You can interview the whole bunch at once. Chrissie lives with my ex and her . . . whatever he is."

"She's not remarried?"

"Nah. That might screw up her alimony."

"If Chrissie's inheriting a house, she must be looking forward to moving out."

"Ah who knows," he snorted. "Then she and her druggie boyfriend might actually have to pay bills. Nah, I imagine Chrissie would sell the house and she and Jerry would party until the cows came home."

I hated the name Jerry, even though Gerry was the Americanized version of my father's name—Geraldo. My father's name, Geraldo Sabala, sounded like flamenco music. Jerry sounded like two thuds on a bass drum.

Rusty stretched forward and picked up the package of Marlboros by the heaping ashtray. "There's just one little hitch with that plan."

"And that is?"

"Me." He lit his cigarette, leaned back, and inhaled deeply, savoring the moment. "My mother misjudged me. She retained me as the executor, expecting me to act like the dutiful little Russell. No matter how she screwed me, I'd still be the good little boy. But, hey, I'm a busy man. If this will holds up, I may not get the damn thing executed for three . . . four years." He smiled wickedly.

CHAPTER 14

Chrissie and family lived on a small street above Escalona on the West Side. The location hinted at ocean views and money, but I still wasn't prepared for the grandeur of the house, a cream-colored Italian style villa that wrapped around a cliff. I could see why Chrissie might not be in a hurry to move out.

Because of its perch on the face of a bluff, the house didn't have a driveway so I pulled my Ghia into a space in front of one of the three garage doors. I mounted broad steps flanked by statues of lions. Etched glass bordered the single oak door to create a more imposing entrance. The doorbell chimed.

This was the first job that I'd brought into Sloan's Investigative Services, so the check in my pocket represented my first official retainer working under a licensed PI. But this case felt odd. Vague. I felt doubtful that what my client wanted me to find actually existed. I could understand why J.J. Sloan preferred straight up homicides.

The woman who answered the door looked about forty and carried a chubby toddler on her hip. She did not look like a harried mom, but like a pampered woman. Tight red Capris declared that the baby had not hurt her shape. She had to lean sideways for the tot to have a place to sit on her slim hips. Layered shoulder-length blond hair glinted with professional highlights and her toenails and fingernails, painted to match the Capris, were spangled with rhinestones.

She cocked her head and raised her eyebrows.

"Melanie Mills?" I asked.

"Yes." Her smooth forehead wrinkled. Door to door solicitors didn't usually know one's name. She glanced past me to the beat up car and looked slightly alarmed.

I frequently toyed with the idea of getting the '66 Ghia a paint job and new upholstery, but I thought the facelift might destroy its character.

The baby, marked as a boy by blue corduroy overalls, inspected my face with round, unblinking blue eyes.

I handed Melanie my business card and gave her a synopsis of the reason for my visit.

"Rusty must be desperate," she said and waved me in.

I'd received more encouraging salutations in my life time. I followed Melanie over the glossy wooden floor of the commodious entryway. The baby slowly rotated his head so the staring eyes never left my face. Staring back, I bugged my eyes.

Bland as an unglazed doughnut, the little boy ratcheted up the intensity of his gaze to a demonic level. The child was clearly possessed. Since I'd never win against the devil, I turned my attention to the living room. Glass doors to the deck and a vista over Santa Cruz dominated the room.

Melanie placed the child on the plush gray carpet littered with baby toys. He twisted on to a haunch so he could continue to inspect me.

"Intent little fellow," I said, as I took a pen and notepad from my purse.

"This is Anthony," Melanie said proudly. She squatted by the baby, shook a small teddy bear in his face, and cooed, "Hi, Anthony. Hi, sweet thing. How's my big boy?"

Blue beams from Hell continued to shoot into my face.

At one time, the baby would have been evidence that Melanie was quite a bit younger than Rusty, but with science rendering the biological clock obsolete, a person never knew. Maybe

Melanie was simply a lot better preserved than Rusty.

Melanie gave up trying to get Anthony's attention and settled on a L-shaped couch upholstered in a tweedy gray and blue. I nabbed a black leather chair.

"I feel bad for Rusty," Melanie said. "I really do." She sank back into the cushions and flung her right leg over her left calling attention to a small rose tattoo. The stem curled around her ankle and the red bud bloomed at the bottom of her calf. Nothing like a tattoo to declare one's self still young and hip.

"Why's that?"

She looked sideways at me, trying to assess whether I knew and was leading her, or whether I were truly ignorant. It didn't matter; the woman was ready to talk. One could get only limited stimulus from shaking a rattle for Anthony or getting another facial.

"Rusty's hurting for money and I gather his mother didn't leave him any or you wouldn't be investigating the will."

I let her words stand. It wasn't my job to tell her about the fifty thousand, which seemed insignificant to Rusty, anyway. "Why does Rusty need money so badly?" In spite of myself, I couldn't stay focused on the will. I thought of the dead Gladys Mills and the unexplained needle mark. Rusty needed money and had expected to inherit.

Melanie crossed her arms and looked askance at me. She really did not believe I didn't know this. "Rusty was the builder of that big development along the coast. The one that was burnt to the ground."

I jotted notes. *So that was Rusty's development.* I was slowly making connections. The apparent arson had been big news. Everyone had suspected greased palms in the approval of the project in the first place. Built on the ocean side of Highway One, the resort development had been much hated both by environmentalists and local residents who'd had their ocean views blocked. When nearly completed, the development had been torched. "How about insurance?"

Melanie shook her head. "Since the fire was clearly arson, the insurance company isn't going to settle until the investigation is complete. That may be never."

Anthony, who'd not stopped scrutinizing me, used the coffee table to pull himself up. The blue satanic headlights inched toward me.

"And it wasn't just the money invested in the resort. The people who burned it caused Mills' Construction to be in the paper, day after day, in a negative light. That's bad for business."

"So you're surprised Gladys didn't help Rusty out?"

"Oh no. When she wanted to be, Gladys was a mean old bitch."

CHAPTER 15

According to Melanie, Gladys had probably cut Rusty out of her will because he'd "put her in a home."

"Sanest thing Rusty ever did," Melanie added. Rusty owned a small guest house behind his own home. "I wouldn't doubt that Rusty needs the rent money. Otherwise, who knows, he might have caved into his mom.

"He's always been too susceptible to his mom's manipulation," Melanie continued. "One reason we're divorced."

Even though we were close in age, I hadn't expected to have anything in common with Melanie Mills, but a manipulative mother-in-law was one of the reasons I'd divorced, too.

Anthony had reached the edge of the table and was drooling. I expected a transmorgrification at any moment with a clawed and fanged creature springing for my neck.

"You've captivated him," the mother remarked.

I couldn't stand it any longer. I reached down, scooped up the kid's plastic key ring, and tossed it over his shoulder. He didn't turn or blink.

The mother giggled as though Anthony's hypnotic, satanic gaze were the cutest little thing.

"Gladys needed to be in a place where people could look after her," Melanie added in Rusty's defense. "Rusty couldn't do that. He's a workaholic. Another reason we're no longer married."

"So Gladys needed someone to keep an eye on her?" I asked hopefully.

Melanie stooped down to retrieve the kid's plastic keys, training wheels for all his future cars and houses and boats. She rattled the keys, trying to get Anthony to turn and stalling for time. Melanie may have been a spoiled, stay-at-home mom, but she wasn't stupid. She considered what hung in the balance of her response. The woman didn't like Gladys, and if Rusty were still paying her alimony, it behooved her to keep him solvent.

Unable to distract her miniature Beelzebub, she asked, "Do you mean like Alzheimer's?"

I shrugged. "Dementia of any type. Mood swings. Depression."

"Generally nuts?"

"Sure."

"I'm no shrink," Melanie said, "but I always thought she was loony."

I wrote her words verbatim. I should have been thinking good, but my feelings were mixed. Rusty was my client, but Gladys had befriended my mom.

"How would you describe your relationship with Rusty?"

Although I didn't know any way that question connected to Gladys's will change, Melanie didn't mind my asking. She shrugged her delicate shoulders. "We get along pretty good for a divorced couple. I waited way too long to get divorced. Rusty's wound pretty tight, and I thought he could go ballistic, but he didn't. Since he's not the demonstrative type, it's hard to know what he's feeling, but we share the kids. We have twin girls and a boy. Great kids. I have them most of the time because Rusty's so busy, but he's supposed to take them every other weekend. That keeps us in communication. When we talk, he's civil. Cooperative."

She was a talker. Lonely, perhaps? Or maybe to her I was

no different than the manicurist. She could gab away because it didn't count. I didn't count.

"How about Gladys? Did you visit Gladys?"

"Of course." She tipped her perfect head of sparkling hair. "She's the children's grandmother. We went every other week." The woman's thumb rubbed her crimson nails.

"What does that have to do with Gladys changing her will? Don't tell me she left everything to me," the woman joked.

A nasty feeling was crawling into my consciousness. One of those ugly creatures that had escaped Pandora's Box. One of the deadly sins. I disliked Melanie simply because she looked great, had a beautiful house and a chubby, complaisant baby that didn't even fuss, all, apparently, without lifting a finger.

"No offense," she continued, "but I feel bad that Rusty has resorted to this." She said this as though it were a hacked up snot ball. Unfortunately this referred to the beater parked in front of her garage and the investigator parked in her leather chair.

"An investigation of the will?" She lifted her pale brows. "He should know better than anyone how Gladys could get in a snit. He should save his money."

"So he can pay you alimony?" *No offense.*

Melanie didn't flinch. She gave me a sardonic smile, amused. I could hear her regaling her friends with the story of Rusty's little PI. Because yes, she probably did have friends, dozens of them, cocktail parties full of them. She rose from the sofa indicating the end of the interview.

No one else was home, Melanie informed me. Rusty and Melanie's children were at school. Melanie's partner, Michael Locatelli, was at work, and Chrissie had been rehired by Harbor View.

"Harbor View must be desperate for help," Melanie quipped as she escorted me to the door. She had, to my relief, left baby Anthony in the living room.

CHAPTER 16

The reception area of Harbor View looked as smooth as it had on my first visit. A huge floral arrangement of fall flowers—gold chrysanthemums and violet and pink asters accented the shiny marble counter. There was no indication of a recent death. Hell, for all I knew, there may have been several recent deaths. This was a large community of the elderly.

Katherine O'Conner, administrator with the hair of steel, manned the front desk. She ranked enough to escape the mauve HVE uniform. Today she sported an ivory silk blouse beneath a dark blue suit.

"Carol Sabala," she greeted me with a practiced smile. This woman was good. "Have you come to pick up your mother?"

"My mother is here?"

The woman was unruffled. She smiled again. "Bea came for a second tour of the facility."

I felt alarmed and guilty at the same time. In my busyness, I hadn't told my mom what I'd learned about Harbor View, its shortage of staff, its suspicious deaths, its Tang instead of juice. I'd assumed that Gladys's death had killed her interest in the place.

"Where is she?" I sounded like a one-person vigilante.

Katherine stood. She was an imposing, straight backed woman. She smiled yet again. "I gather, then, that you are here on other business. Could I help you with that?"

I took a breath. My mother's connection to Harbor View

was a good thing in terms of investigation. I simply could never allow her to live here.

"I need to talk to Chrissie Locatelli."

"May I ask what this regards?"

I pulled out a business card and handed it to her. "Rusty Mills hired me," I explained.

The woman flicked the corner of the card with her thumbnail. I posed a dilemma: the investigator for a man who planned a lawsuit vs. the daughter of a potential client. Her mysteriously smooth face remained unfurrowed, but the card clicked like a Geiger counter. Then it stopped. "You'll have to talk to Chrissie Locatelli somewhere else."

"Okay. If you tell me when she has her break, I'll talk to her somewhere else."

"You don't understand," Katherine said with a faint smile. "I'm not trying to stonewall you. Chrissie doesn't work here anymore."

Katherine may not have been trying to give me a hard time, but she was a little too happy to impart this news. "Chrissie's mom told me that I would find Chrissie here."

"Chrissie was let go this morning."

Let go. What a strange euphemism. As though it were liberating to be fired. "Why?"

The woman shook her head. Confidential. Against policy. Katherine struck me as a person who lived her life according to policy. I'd get the information elsewhere.

"I'm going to talk to my mother," I said. "I'm sure she'd appreciate a ride home. Could you tell me where I could find her?"

Katherine looked as though she'd prefer to come around the counter and toss me on the curb except that would be against policy. "Your mother stopped to offer Ida Walker her condolences and last I knew, the two were in Ida's room chatting."

I could feel the woman's eyes watching me down the hallway.

I turned into the long corridor to Ida's room; Jack Dorfman wobbled toward me from the far end. He was singing. "If Ida Walker, I'd walk in the morning. I'd walk in the evening, all over this land."

If he had a walker, he could certainly walk faster. Even though I had twice the distance to cover, I arrived at Ida's door well before Jack. I knocked and rested my back on the wall. I'd be damned if the old codger were going to fondle my ass again. *Fool me once, shame on you. Fool me twice, shame on me.*

"Hey, beautiful," Jack greeted me as Ida opened the door.

Ida coquettishly tucked a strand of white hair behind her ear. Then I stepped away from the wall and ruined the moment.

"It's a party!" Jack announced, swaying broad hips behind his black cane. "Round up Bea and let's go."

My mom was making friends here. This was not good.

"Are you going to join us, dumpling?" Jack asked me as Ida disappeared into her room.

I backed against the wall.

"We're going to a strip club," Jack announced.

If there were a strip club in the area, I might have believed Jack was going, but not accompanied by my mom. Besides, it was only five thirty – dinnertime.

Ida and my mom emerged from Ida's room. "Look, Bea," Jack exclaimed, "your daughter's here to visit you and you're not even a resident yet."

My mom looked pained. Couldn't she have a little fun with friends without me checking up on her? The entourage started down the corridor at the pace of a banana slug.

"Why don't you come and eat with us?" Ida chirped.

My mom squirmed as though her blue blouse were itchy. The color did nothing to offset her pallor. I felt bad that I hadn't followed through more since our visit to Dr. Jellinek, but now did not seem like the time to inquire about her health.

"They make a dynamite macaroni and cheese," Jack Dorfman chortled.

My mouth salivated. I liked macaroni and cheese, and since I started work at four in the morning, the old folks' eating schedule of lunch at twelve and supper at five thirty suited me.

Jack fell in line beside my mom. I prayed he would try his stunt with her; that would turn her off to Harbor View.

At least, I hoped it would. Maybe in Santa Cruz, my mom's sexual appetites would become as spicy as her culinary tastes.

"You could tell us what you found out about Gladys," Ida plied.

Over Ida's tiny frame, I could see my mom shriveling like one of the witches on The Wizard of Oz.

"The state has to look into Gladys's death." I glanced past my mom to see if Jack Dorfman's free hand were still in a proper place.

"Hey," Jack Dorfman boomed from the end of the line. He'd been out of the spotlight for thirty seconds and, dammit, that was long enough. "Did you hear O.J. is going to get married again?"

He paused on his cane. Big, craggy, bent over. Three women stopped and looked at him.

"He's gonna take another stab at it."

Ida tittered. My mom and I smiled. I'd heard the joke last year.

We resumed our shuffle down the carpet. The song It's a Long Road to Tipperary popped into my skull. I substituted macaroni for Tipperary.

"Do any of you know why Chrissie was fired?" I asked.

"Chrissie was fired?" Ida echoed. "I thought she lost her job when Gladys died?"

"Harbor View rehired her."

"Well I'll be hanged." Jack Dorfman halted and scratched his gray border of hair. "They must be desperate for workers."

"Why do you say that?" I asked.

"Well look at her," he said, as though that explained everything.

He seemed to envision her himself because he mused, "She did have a nice little rumpus."

My mom looked at him in amazement.

"Get used to it, Bea," Ida quipped. "Jack has an obsession with asses."

Jack smiled, not at all abashed. "What's not to like?" He peered over my mom at Ida. "Do you know little Tomás?"

Ida shook her head.

The group seemed incapable of walking and talking at the same time.

"You know. The young guy who brings around the meds."

"I don't get any meds," Ida snapped.

Except your shots, I thought.

"You've seen him with the cart," Jack insisted. "He comes down the hallway every day. The kid with curly hair?"

Ida shook her head. "They all look like kids to me."

Jack let out a long, lugubrious sigh. "Big smile. Perfect teeth." Jack illustrated the big smile with a mouthful of crooked gray teeth.

Ida shook her head again.

Jack gawked at her, not believing Ida's story. His big nose twitched.

My mom sniffed the air. "Something smells good," she said, reminding them of dinner. Her complexion was pallid. I wanted to scream, "Get this woman some food!" but settled for mouthing over the top of Ida's head, "Are you okay?"

In response, my mom glowered. *Did I think I was her mother?*

Jack and Ida unlocked horns and we resumed our trudge down the hall.

"So does Tomás have something to do with Chrissie?" I asked. I hoped he didn't connect to Jack's fanny fetish.

"He's the one who accused Chrissie of stealing meds from the cart," Jack said. "Actually, it was my Darvon. That's why Harbor View fired her the first time."

"Do any of you know where I could find Chrissie now?"

"Bea, is your daughter a state investigator?" Ida asked.

"Carol is a private investigator," my mom announced proudly.

A warm pain trickled through my chest, the sensation of a heart melting.

Until that moment, I'd never imagined my mom was proud of me.

CHAPTER 17

Tomás Garcia looked all of seventeen. His smallness added to the sense he was a kid. Nonetheless, he was intent and serious about loading medication from the storage room to the cart. His tag identified him as a medical technician.

Even though I'd given Tomás my card, he was watchful of me, but to get medicines from the shelves, he had to turn away. Even with little experience as a thief, I could have swiped some pills from the cart with no problem.

"So you accused Chrissie Locatelli of stealing meds?" I asked. I was clearly outside the parameters of my investigation, but I couldn't help myself.

"I didn't accuse her of anything. I *saw* her snag Mr. Dorfman's Darvon."

"What did you do?"

"I told our new administrator—Ms. O'Conner." Tomás spoke with softened T's, without the full thud of the D, a hint of his ancestry more than an accent. "Missing meds have to be reported to the state."

From the closet-like room, Tomás shook pills from prescription bottles and placed them in labeled cups.

"I don't see any cup for Mr. Dorfman."

"His Darvon is on request. He takes it when his leg is aching." Tomás smiled briefly at the thought of Jack Dorfman, giving me a glimpse of the perfect teeth. "He says the pins in his leg pick up television signals and they ache whenever there's a rerun of Family Ties."

From a large bottle, Tomás poured pills on to a tray. With a plastic wand, he whisked five into a cup, counting softly to himself, and slid the remainder back into their container.

"So Mr. Dorfman had what? Maybe one? Darvon in his cup."

Tomás stopped his work and snapped to attention. His shoulders shot up under the mauve HVE shirt. He may have been young and petite, but he had a straight spine and direct brown eyes. "That's only the medication I saw her take. We've been having a problem for a while. Whole bottles of missing Vicodin and Percocet."

"How could that happen?" I asked innocently. "The bottles stay here. The room is locked, I presume."

"Of course."

"But sometimes it is accidentally left unlocked," I stated.

His eyes narrowed. "What makes you say that?"

"Citations are a matter of public record."

That may have been so, but Tomás didn't buy for a moment that I'd looked up Harbor View Estates' records, and one of Leonard's complaints had been that the facility didn't post its citations as required by law.

Still, Tomás was not about to take the blame. "The key hangs on a hook in a little office we have for staff."

"So anyone could have borrowed it?"

Tomás looked away.

I imagined the theft was even easier than that. Lock or no lock would hardly make a difference to a young, cute girl like Chrissie. She could flirt her way into the small storage room and lift a bottle right behind Tomás's back.

"Did Mr. Glass, the state licensing investigator, ever question you about the missing drugs?"

"No." Tomás took my card out of his shirt pocket and scanned it again.

"Do you have any idea where I could find Chrissie Locatelli?"

"If she's not at home, she's probably hanging out on the mall with her boyfriend."

"Jerry?"

He nodded curtly.

"I take it you know him."

He returned my business card to the pocket of his shirt. "We were in high school together."

"Was he a druggie then?"

Tomás shrugged. "I don't think so. He was a decent student. Played baseball. He was fast, a good base stealer, but he never had much power."

He didn't disclaim Jerry was a druggie now. Tomás locked the door, deposited the key in the pocket of his slacks, and pointedly checked his watch. "I have to make my rounds." He pushed the cart down the hallway.

I trotted beside him. "I'd like to talk to you some more."

"I see by your card that you're not with state licensing, so why are you here?" Tomás asked.

I told him.

"I tell you what," he said. "If you want to talk to me later about Chrissie or Jerry, fine. But I don't see how Gladys Mills' will has anything to do with Harbor View. If you have questions about the facility, you need to talk to the administrator."

He rapped at a partially opened door decorated with a big wreath of grape vine and dried statice. "Mrs. Johnson," he called. "It's me, Tomás. Time for your medicine."

I headed for the exit, but turned to see if Tomás had pushed the cart into the room. It stood unattended outside the door, a pill addict's smorgasbord on wheels.

CHAPTER 18

The mewling of a kitten in trauma filled the hallway. Anyone else may have been alarmed, but I knew it was my stomach. *Damn that Jack Dorfman and his mention of macaroni and cheese.* The aroma filled the air.

I paced up and down the carpeted hallways looking for a pay phone, but didn't find any. I could hardly ask Katherine O'Conner to use the phone at the reception area for the call I needed to make.

I reluctantly headed for the cafeteria. My mom was ensconced in Gladys's chair. She looked at home with Ida, Harriet and Jack. *This was not a good thing.*

"So you changed your mind," Jack said, already looking about the table for a way to squeeze me in.

Saliva pooled in my mouth at the sight of the mounds of macaroni and cheese, but I shook my head and asked Ida if I could use her phone.

My mom gave me a baleful look.

"Certainly, dear," Ida said, handing me her room key. "Just don't snoop around for any evidence,"she said with a smile.

When I entered Ida's apartment, I thought about how different a room felt when not occupied by its inhabitant. All the furniture dimmed, as though the couch, the refrigerator, the table reflected Ida's life, and without Ida, they became inert objects, and I noticed for the first time that the table was blue and Ida's phone was clunky and ivory, one step up from a rotary.

I called David. With itchy frustration, I listened to the phone ring and then the answering machine pick up. "This is your wonderful, sweet, precious Carol, the one you adore," I started, before I begged him to find out if Harbor View had ever reported missing medication.

After hanging up, I looked around Ida's apartment. On the wall over the table, she had two big photos of her and her husband, one when they were young, possibly newlyweds, and one with a cake indicating a celebration of their golden wedding anniversary. Her husband was a suave man with silver hair and a silver mustache.

I meandered into the kitchen area and inspected the photos on Ida's refrigerator. They were recent photos from Harbor View, all meticulously labeled. Halloween, 1995. Christmas, 1995. Mildred on her birthday.

Mildred Levine? I wondered. *How common was the name Mildred?* The photo showed a toad of a woman in a wheelchair with a birthday cap strung around blue-gray hair.

After I returned Ida's key and thanked her profusely so my mom wouldn't think she'd raised a heathen, I headed to my car. Having left a world of canes and walkers, I felt thankful for my long galloping legs. *I can kill two birds with one stone*, I thought as I plopped into the cracked driver's seat. I groaned aloud and massaged my eyebrows. *Was I ever going to be free of my mother's maxims? Was her voice going to ride around inside me like some sort of life-long pregnancy?*

I drove to downtown Santa Cruz. Tomás had said if Chrissie weren't home, she'd be on the mall with her boyfriend. "On the mall" meant Chrissie liked to hang out on Pacific Avenue, the main street through Santa Cruz's coffee houses, clothing shops and book stores. I found parking behind Palace Arts and cut through the store to the sidewalk.

Chrissie was exactly where I expected to find her. Outside the Coffee Roasting Company, she leaned on the rail around the tables, a collection spot for the street urchins of Santa Cruz.

The age of the congregation reminded me of Annabel Heather Smith, a nude model I'd met on my last case. She was too clean cut for this crowd. Such a pretty girl. My throat stopped at the thought of Annie.

To collect myself, I stared at ballet slippers in the window of Jackson's Shoes. That only provoked an image of a little Annie in a pink tutu.

The next window of Dell Williams Jewelry Store made the welling emotion worse with its display of sentimental Lladró figurines, sweet little girls pressed to their mother's skirts. My stomach growled. I took a deep breath and turned back to the twilight scene and my task at hand.

The girl with Chrissie had short raven hair and wore boots with thick square heels, much more substantial than her halter top and mini skirt. She had multiple rings in her eyebrow and a ring in her nose. She dramatically flung her cigarette to the sidewalk and talked loudly about her "fucking mother." With burnt out eyes, she watched me approach.

At least you have a mother, I thought. No one had mentioned Chrissie's mother. Life without a dad was familiar territory to me, but I couldn't imagine life without a mom. Even if I'd preferred cowboy boots to ballet slippers, even though my mom was not the type to cuddle me against her side, having a mother comforted me in a deep, primal way, like being rocked in a cradle.

"Hi, Chrissie."

The girl spun around. "Oh, fuck, you scared me."

The raven-haired friend chortled at Chrissie's surprise.

"It's you." Chrissie's voice was slurred, her pupils constricted. "The Martini Lady."

"Can I talk to you for a minute?" I took advantage of Chrissie's dazed confusion. "I'll buy you something to eat."

Chrissie turned nervous eyes to her friend.

The girl shrugged. Her thin arms dangled, allowing a clear view of a nasty, infected bruise on the inside of her left elbow. She'd gone for an easy, obvious vein and botched the job. "Go ahead. I'll hang here," the girl said.

I fought to reign in judgment. A year ago a couple of street kids had saved my life. They hadn't intended to, but nonetheless they had, and I'd decided never to malign the coterie again.

Chrissie followed me into the narrow, deep coffee house, the grout of the rough tile black with grime and spilled drinks and the air redolent with fresh ground beans. We stood in line in front of the curving, vaguely Deco counter.

"What do you want?" Chrissie asked sullenly.

"I think I'll have some vegetarian chili."

The girl rolled her eyes like a fourteen-year-old. I wondered if that was when she'd started self-medicating, numbing her emotional growth. A stain ran down the front of her pink scooped neck tee-shirt. She wiped at it, scratched her arms, and stared out the window.

"What happened there?"

"Vomit."

"Are you sick?"

She snorted at that, as though it were a joke.

The short line had deposited us before the cash register and I ordered my meal. "Want anything?"

Chrissie asked for three large café lattes. Then she wandered away from me and inspected the desserts in the glass case.

I hoped she didn't plan on dessert, too. I only had a twenty. "Let's sit down," I suggested, sliding into one of the high backed wooden booths.

After several minutes, she deigned to follow suit.

"Is one of the coffee drinks for Jerry?"

She didn't answer.

I handed her my card. She glanced at it, folded it, and dropped it on the floor.

"I want to talk to you about Gladys."

The girl's face crumpled, the dark brows pulled together, the lips disappeared, the eyes teared. The three espresso drinks touched down on the counter. She jumped up to gather them. Then she walked out.

CHAPTER 19

A moment later the steaming bowl of chili was plonked on the glass display case and my name was called. I told myself that Chrissie had just gone to give her friend a latte. I hesitated long enough that when I went out to the sidewalk, Chrissie had slipped into the twilight.

Her dark-haired friend lounged on the railing. She clutched two lattes to her scrawny chest and smirked with bright red lips.

"Is that other drink for Jerry?"

"Spare change?" she asked tonelessly, as though I were a complete stranger.

"Information?"

She glanced furtively at the group, four guys and a heavy set girl on the other side of the entrance. They'd been approached by a tall, scraggly-haired man with burnt, tough skin and stiff clothes. The young guys enthusiastically greeted him with complicated handshakes.

Miss Raven Hair took a sip of her drink and looked anxiously at the man. The coarse skin and untamed hair and beard made him look fifty, but he could easily have been thirty-five.

"How much?" she whispered. Her eyes flicked to the street person with a look between desperation and lust. She licked her lips and took another sip of coffee.

Ah, the dilemma. If I were a real PI, I would have stuffed my pockets with bribery money. As it was, I'd spent almost all of my only twenty on three drinks and the bowl of chili, growing cold on the counter.

"Twenty," I said.

She extended her middle and index fingers.

"I'll have to pay you later."

She gave me a look of disgust. "You are so lame." She dumped the spare coffee down the front of my Levi's and on to my Converse high tops.

Fortunately, the humiliation was lukewarm. I felt like strangling the bitch.

She sauntered her skinny ass over to her buddies, hulking lads with shaved heads who smiled at the impromptu theater.

An older couple at the outdoor tables had looked on with mild alarm. I walked inside and grabbed some napkins to sop up the mess.

The female half of the couple waddled into the coffee house. She was gray-haired and kind-faced. "Are you okay?"

"Yeah, fine." I bit back the anger. "Just an accident."

I asked the girl at the counter to nuke my chili and then I settled down on one of the stools near the window where I could watch the Pacific Avenue drama from the safety of the Coffee Roasting Company. It was a long intermission. My chili was gone and my wet leg was thoroughly chilled before the action resumed.

I assumed the guy joining the assembly was Jerry. He was a surprise. For starters, he had hair, brown hair, cut conservatively, like a guy from the early Sixties, but with a little spikiness. He had no visible tattoos or piercings, but then his arms were covered by a dress shirt, tucked neatly into a pair of jeans. He looked like someone who'd gotten off work.

Miss Raven Hair became animated, gesticulating with her cigarette toward me. I watched the mime of the coffee pouring. She curled over her cigarette with laughter. Jerry smiled grimly and glanced in my direction.

I waved.

He said something to the group and they moved slowly, like an amebic organism.

I exited the back of the coffee house, through the cantina of El Palomar restaurant, into an enclosed walkway of shops and out into the parking lot. By the time I maneuvered the Ghia around to Pacific Avenue, the band had dissolved into the night.

CHAPTER 20

When I drove up to my pinkish abode, Lola padded out to greet me, shrieking that she'd been abandoned. It was the truth. I had not thought about her all day. Thank God I wasn't a mother. I'd be one of those who forgot her baby in the car and let it bake to a crisp.

My first priority, before I opened the door, before I relieved my bladder, was to scratch behind Lola's freckled ear.

"You are The Best Cat in the Universe," I purred to her.

She nuzzled my hand and purred her assent.

"I'm so glad you're not a drug addict."

A horn blasted. I whirled and Lola ripped through the dark and scrabbled over the fence.

A dark pickup was parked in front of Mrs. Bloom's house and Rusty Mills was clambering from its cab. He tossed something back on to the seat, probably his trusty bottle of Maalox. Mrs. Bloom peeked around the edge of her curtain. She claimed to have visions. Maybe this was one of them.

Rusty slammed the squeaking door. "Hey, there," he greeted me. "I've been trying to reach you all day. Since you never, apparently, check in at your office, I thought I'd try here."

In addition to resembling his mom in appearance and chain smoking, Rusty also possessed Gladys's disregard for boundaries. He should not have been here, at my house.

He strode purposefully across the U of the cul-de-sac as though he were on his site, king of the subdivision.

It was a balmyr night but I felt chilled in my wet jeans. The palm tree rustled. "How did you get my address?"

Rusty chortled. He coughed, thumped his chest, and spat. "Dust," he explained.

"How did you find out where I live?"

"As a private investigator, you must know how easy that is." It could be easy, but since I'd been tracked to my house before, I tried to make it hard. My home phone was unlisted. My card gave only my work number. The office included J.J., me and an answering machine, and J.J. was less likely than the machine to give out my home address.

I was glad to see Mrs. Bloom's face in the light of her window, the lace curtain like a mantilla.

"So what's up?" I asked, trying to sound casual.

"I wanted a status report."

"Your ex-wife thinks your mom changed the will out of plain old meanness," I said bluntly.

"Yeah, I know." He shrugged, the chest and shoulders massive under his tee-shirt. "I talked to her. Something I forgot to tell you about Melanie. Anything that goes in her ears, goes out her mouth."

"She'd probably be willing to step up and testify your mom was nuts," I said.

Instead of smiling, Rusty tensed, his hands balling into fists.

I threw my arms into the air. "Hey, did I miss something here? I thought this was the kind of stuff I was after."

He shook himself out, like a boxer trying to get his muscles to relax. "Just a natural male response to a 'Your mama' statement." He smiled.

I didn't smile. My client gave me the creeps. In my insulated job as a baker, I didn't have much contact with people. I didn't face this dilemma of professionalism vs. unpleasant client on a regular basis.

I gave Rusty a terse report on my attempt to find and talk to Chrissie.

He glanced at his watch. "Why don't you call her at home?"

I clenched my teeth. Maybe it was better to be a baker. At Archibald's, people trusted me to do my job. "That's a good idea," I said, walking over to my mailbox.

"Don't blow me off, Carol," Rusty Mills growled. He grabbed me by the shoulder. I spun, crouched, ready to kick into his shin. "Whoa, Nellie," he said. This time he was the one to throw his hands in the air and back away.

"It's not a good idea to grab women outside in the dark." Maybe I should carry my gun. My nice, simple revolver that I kept in a locked drawer.

"Let's go inside then," Rusty Mills suggested.

Not on your life. "Look, I'll call Chrissie tonight, but I don't expect her to be home. It looked like a party night to me."

"At her boyfriend's place?"

"I suppose," I grumbled. *Why did he need me to find her? He seemed to know more about her than I did.* As Gladys had put it, they were practically kin, with Rusty's ex-wife living with Chrissie's dad.

"When you find her, I want to know *everything* she says." He underscored the word in the air. "Not just about the will. Everything." He turned abruptly and stalked back to his truck.

CHAPTER 21

My cat was not the only one feeling neglected. I had three phone messages from David.

The first one said: Where are you?

The second one said: What about my needs?

The third one said: How about a bike ride tomorrow?

He didn't respond to my question on his answering machine about Harbor View Estates reporting missing medication. As much as I wanted to pick up the phone and call David on the spot, I peeled off my damp jeans and reeking tee shirt and climbed into the shower. Rusty Mills' visit had left me feeling as though my body were coated with construction dust and smoke fumes.

Wrapped in my long terry cloth robe, my hair in a towel, I dragged the phone from my bedroom to my office and made the first call. At the same time, I opened Word to start a new case file.

On the third ring, a friendly male voice answered. I identified myself.

Chrissie was not at home, he said, but I might try her boyfriend's house. Did I have the number?

The voice caressed me, warm, respectful, helpful, an antidote to a day of degradation, like a shot of quality whiskey. I was in love.

I flirted a little, told him he had the voice for a radio announcer. *For phone sex* was what I really had in mind.

He flirted back, said he was fascinated by a woman working as a private investigator. He seemed unconcerned about his daughter, Chrissie Locatelli, but then she was twenty-something.

I asked for Jerry's address and he gave it to me, as well as the kid's last name: Vargas.

"Nice kid," he said. "I hope some of it rubs off on Chrissie."

Jerry Vargas. I rolled the name around on my tongue. It was a name like mine that spoke of being an Americanized Mexican or a half breed.

"Is there anything else I can do for you?"

I could think of a few things.

"Where does Jerry work?"

"Stewart's Pharmacy. He's a clerk."

I called David Shapiro.

"Where have you been?" His voice was full of impatience and Woody Allen whine.

Before I could explain, he said, "Why don't you come over?"

"I have work to do."

"Work is for fools and mules."

I tamped down my anger. David worked half-time and I worked double time. Plus he gloated. This was surely a match made in hell.

Good investments allowed David to be semi-retired. His smug position, not any revolutionary philosophy, allowed for his cavalier attitude toward work. And the attitude was mostly part of his persona, pulled out now to badger me. He'd shown his true colors with his recent lecture about endangering his job.

"I don't hear any 'Sure, honey, I'd love to run over and satisfy your needs.'"

"I'm trying to decide whether I'm a fool or a mule."

"Ah, Carol, I'm just being my usual jerky self. You're not going to work more tonight, are you? It's ten o'clock. This is supposed to be your day off."

It was a few minutes past nine. And I was contemplating drying my hair and driving to Jerry's house.

"Don't you have to go to work at four?" he pressed.

"All the more reason not to come over."

"Then how about a bike ride tomorrow?" His voice was thick with disappointment. We'd passed the honeymoon stage of our relationship and entered the period of issues. Which house would we choose or would we continue to live apart? How would we deal with the inequity in our schedules? If we couldn't resolve these issues, they were big enough to pull us apart and we both knew it.

When the silence had expanded to a few seconds, he said, "I have some news for you."

"About the case?"

"About the case," he mimicked sarcastically. "Listen to you. Suddenly you're interested. Sorry to disappoint you, but the news is that I have prostate cancer."

"You do not."

"How do you know?"

"If you had prostate cancer, you would hardly be proposing a bike ride tomorrow."

David was right, though. News of the case arrested my attention; he used my guilt and excitement to extort a bike ride for the next day.

CHAPTER 22

Jerry Vargas lived in "affordable housing," a run-down string of apartments off Ocean Avenue. The doors opened onto the asphalt driveway. Not a very safe place for children.

Either nobody had a porch light or they didn't work, so the numbers weren't visible. Not a problem. I headed toward the end, a lit window and the sound of music. After a year with David Shapiro, I didn't even think of it as loud. I also recognized Sponge. What did that mean that I had a middle-aged boyfriend who listened to the same music as post-adolescent druggies?

The road into the complex continued around the apartment and was edged by overgrown shrubs.

I rapped on splintered wood. Knocking on an unfamiliar door held the same excitement as tearing the wrapping from an unexpected gift.

"Turn it down, Phil," someone yelled.

Jerry Vargas peered around the side of thick drapes, and must have decided I didn't look threatening. He cracked the door. "Can I help you?" he asked politely. He didn't seem to recognize me from the coffee house. He still wore his dress shirt. His eyes looked clear and undilated. He didn't smell of alcohol or betray any sign there might be a party going on.

Maybe Jerry only supplied drugs. Maybe he was a designated driver. Maybe I was completely wrong. Maybe the party had migrated elsewhere.

I handed Jerry my card. "I'm looking for Chrissie Locatelli."

His glance back into the room told me that she was there. Not that I should have been concerned about Jerry hiding her. The sound of my voice unleashed a string of profanity from Chrissie that came hurtling toward the door. Chrissie Locatelli grabbed Jerry by the shoulder and pulled him backward.

"You fucking Martini bitch!" she yelled. "This is fucking harassment."

Jerry yanked on the door. He did not want me seeing into the room. The edge of the door slammed into Chrissie's shoulder.

Chrissie slapped him on the head. "That fucking hurt."

"Chill out, Chrissie."

She slapped his head again. "Chill out," she mimicked him. "I'm not fucking going to chill out. This bitch is stalking me, harassing me."

One of the bald guys appeared behind her. He looked like a police mug shot. His eyes were cold and his forehead furrowed. He was young enough to be my son, but I was afraid of him.

He grabbed Chrissie's thin wrist. She flailed and pointed at me with her free hand. "I'll tell my dad. He'll fucking sue you. He's the president of Nature's Granola."

The guy with the shaved head clamped Chrissie's other wrist like a handcuff. This served only to make her hop up and down like a pogo stick and cuss a blue streak, some aimed at Jerry, some at me, and some at Curt. She acted like a person on meth, not like someone on a narcotic pain killer like Vicodin or Demerol.

"Your father is the one who gave me this address," I said calmly.

The news deflated Chrissie so quickly and thoroughly that I instantly regretted saying it. She collapsed like a rag doll against the hulk's shoulder and he led her away from my view.

President of Nature's Granola explained the West Side mansion and why Michael Locatelli's name had seemed familiar. Nature's Granola was part of the local mythology, two hippies who roasted their own oats and puffed wheat and honey and cashews, and simply by putting out a tasty product at a fair price had gradually built an empire that now included a whole line of breakfast cereals and health bars.

"I just need to ask Chrissie some questions about her former employer?"

"Gladys Mills? That old sow?" Jerry pulled the door to his body, standing in the crack of dim light.

"Why an old sow?"

Jerry's smooth face puffed with indignation. The soft lips curled petulantly. "Gladys liked to portray herself as Chrissie's fairy godmother, but she wasn't even nice to her. She bossed her around like a servant."

I clamped my teeth and didn't point out that Chrissie had been hired as a personal assistant, nothing more than a nice name for a servant.

"Chrissie only stayed because Gladys paid attention to her. Unlike her family."

"So all I want is to ask Chrissie a couple of questions about Gladys."

His eyes narrowed. "I don't think Chrissie is in any condition to talk to you."

I liked this kid, who seemed way too sweet to be with Chrissie.

"I'd say she's messed up," I remarked.

He shrugged.

"You didn't, by any chance, supply the drugs?"

Even in the minimal light from the room, I could see Jerry blanch.

The stone-faced kid with the shaved head muscled up behind Jerry.

"Back off, Curt. Let me handle this."

Baldy did not back off.

Someone turned the music up. *I hope my head will heal/it's all I ever wanted to feel.*

"Working at a pharmacy," I said to Jerry. "Fine pill selection."

"I've been working there for years," Jerry said defensively.

"Maybe you've just started the stealing. Wanting to keep your girlfriend happy."

The eyes shifted back into the room.

"I can check at Stewart's Pharmacy. See if they're missing any inventory."

"Knock yourself out," he said, still not looking at me. He shut the door. No slamming. No rant. Simple dismissal. I was easier to turn away than a child selling Girl Scout Cookies.

I took one flat-footed step down to the driveway and decided to see what was in the back. Maybe peep in a window.

The shrubbery rustled. Before I could turn, a body rushed at me like a football tackle. The impact hit my lower back and I flew forward. My hands slid and shredded as I sprawled on to the asphalt.

The assailant threw a blanket over my head, kneeled on my arms and in spite of my best bucking and kicking and thrashing, tied the material around my neck.

Footsteps fled. A car started. It sounded like a truck. I struggled to my feet and shuffled cautiously across the road until I ran into the bushes. The last thing I needed now was to be run over, too. The truck roared by me.

I tugged at the cord around my neck, a thick, nylon string. It was not tight. The attacker had not meant to strangle me or to run over me. The truck had not veered, or turned or backed up to hit me. My palms burned and blood dripped down my wrists, but I was not seriously hurt.

This had been intimidation. Curt? I wondered. Clearly not Jerry or Chrissie. The person had knocked me down and pinned me with ease.

I turned the nylon tie until I found the knot. Listening to the muffled song of Sponge, I picked at the knot with my fingernails and had it undone in a couple of minutes.

The fabric was dark and scratchy, not meant for clothing or a blanket. I bundled it into my arms and slunk toward my Ghia.

CHAPTER 23

Bread covered with seeds was all the rage, so on my stainless steel bakery table, I had lined up bags of poppy seeds, fennel seeds, sesame seeds and sunflower seeds.

Eldon, the kitchen manager, appeared over my shoulder like an apparition. He was a huge, pudgy man, well over six feet, who reminded me of the Pillsbury Dough Boy. If you poked him in the middle, he probably would giggle. His essentially amiable and kind personality made his insufferable blathering all the worse; I couldn't tell a person like that to take a hike, a good thing, since Eldon was my boss.

"The bread smells great." He elaborately sniffed the air. "Sourdough?"

Eldon knew damn good and well it was sourdough. If he didn't know it from the menu plans, then he knew it from the fragrance before he'd glided into my cubicle. He had the nose of a bloodhound.

"Uh, what happened to your hands?"

"I fell."

He gazed at the gauze and tape and knew that he wouldn't get any more out of me. "Be sure to wear your gloves."

"What's up, Eldon?" I didn't relish his chit chat. Two of my fingers felt as though they'd never bend again and the bruising around the scraped skin ached.

He crossed his arms over his white chef's smock and sighed. "Well, as you know, Carol, you are a terrific baker.

You have set the bar."

Whenever a boss begins a conversation by complimenting you extravagantly, you know you're in trouble. I had a feeling this conversation was bound down a path we'd traveled before.

"Your bread is so light. When you're not here, customers notice the difference. They comment on it."

This part was unadulterated bullshit. I worked a normal five days a week and the other two days various kitchen personnel filled in as baker. Sometimes Eldon himself baked, and as a graduate of the Culinary Academy of San Francisco, he could outbake me any day. Given the opportunity, Eldon could trounce the Iron Chef. So I couldn't imagine anyone complaining about my absence. I knew where this conversation was leading.

Eldon settled his ample bottom, encased in the houndstooth check pants that didn't flatter anyone's derriere, against the stainless steel table. "It's been my contention for some time that we need to be able to offer this same quality of baked goods seven days a week."

"Listen, Eldon, if you make me a part-time employee, you may as well fire me."

"I think we should revisit some of the possibilities," he said blandly, ignoring my outburst.

"I hate that word *revisit*." As irritating as I found Eldon, he was a perfect kitchen manager—a competent chef, a born bureaucrat, and a calm bearer of bad tidings.

"I will do everything possible to preserve your full-time status, Carol."

"In other words, you've already made up your mind to hire another baker."

Eldon exhaled deeply. He and I both knew that he was being much nicer than he needed to be. It was his kitchen and he could run it as he saw fit. The owner of Archibald's was an out-of-state conglomerate and as long as Eldon and the managers of the other aspects of the conference center turned a profit, they had full run of the place. Eldon could hire whomever he pleased, and if I pissed him off, he could "let me go." I could be liberated like little Chrissie. "Since the person will share your space, I thought you might like to participate in the interviewing process."

So he had already made up his mind and this was his olive branch of *inclusiveness*, another delicious word in the lexicon of managers.

I shrugged, still angry, but I didn't want to cut off my nose to spite my face. "Oh, God," I groaned. There was my mom again, her maxim-filled voice inside of my thoughts.

If there were to be a second baker, it was definitely in my best interest to interview him or her.

"Why don't I just train Ray?" I offered.

"He's been trained," Eldon said flatly, "to be a sous chef. He's much better there than as a baker. Have you ever sampled the muffins when he's filled in for you?"

I took it from Eldon's tone that the muffins were less than promising.

"Ray makes the same mistake most people make. He overmixes." Eldon began a dissertation on How To Avoid Doughy Muffins.

I tuned out and rolled around in my self pity. Ray had recently married and his new wife was pregnant. Eldon assumed as a single person with no kids, I should flex. It wasn't fair. No one asked people to have kids; they chose their fate, but they acted like single people should accommodate the offspring, shelling out money to include baby care on group insurance policies, politely ignoring screaming kids who ruined their dinners out, or caring there was a Baby On Board. I was in a sour mood.

"Folks hang on to the belief that batter has to be smooth," Eldon concluded.

I sighed. "I know you might think with my second job that I don't need a full-time job here, but I'm hardly making anything as a PI." One more reason that I had second thoughts about my newfound career. "It's important to me that you not cut my hours."

Eldon lifted himself away from the table. "Well then," he said, "it's important to the kitchen that you don't ask to cut your hours."

As Eldon left the bakery, I realized that he wanted a back-up baker because he feared I was making a career change. Eldon's uncanny foresight constantly amazed me. I didn't know where private investigation would take me; I avoided the thought. On the other hand, Eldon was already planning for it to take me away.

CHAPTER 24

The Forest of Nisene Marks State Park was not my favorite ride, but I wanted to appease David.

"So this is the only way I can get face time with you?" he'd greeted me. "By pimping information from Leonard?" He'd stomped around loading my bike behind his on the back of his station wagon.

He was too angry to have any sympathy for my scraped hands.

In deference to his feelings, I hadn't whined about his trail choice or pumped him for the information. I deserved a more gracious greeting. We didn't talk much on the short drive to our neighboring town of Aptos.

I mulled over the call I'd made to Chrissie after work. Melanie had answered. Chrissie wasn't home. She'd probably spent the night at Jerry's. The woman had seemed completely unconcerned. But why should she care? Chrissie was of legal age. Chrissie wasn't her daughter. And God only knew, if Chrissie lived in my house, I'd be glad to have her gone, too.

David parked at the entrance of the park to avoid paying the fee, which meant we'd be eating plumes of dust from cars for several miles of our ride. At this time of year, Nisene Marks' fire road was a trail of fine, pulverized dirt.

Still pissed, David shot off ahead of me.

There were lots of things I didn't like about this ride. First of all, it ran through a forest of second-growth redwoods. The first growth had been sacrificed by Loma Prieta Lumber Company to the Southern Pacific Railroad. Nonetheless, the new batch of redwoods had been growing since The Twenties and towered above us, creating a shady, gloomy path. I liked to be in the sun.

David turned off the road on to a single track trail.

"This is hikers only," I shouted at him, but he already knew that.

"If you want to eat dust, be my guest," he shouted over his shoulder. "I'm watching out for hikers."

We returned to the fire road in time to cross a steel bridge and to see the sign. I stopped to read it as I did every time: Epicenter Area, 7.1 Earthquake, 5:04 PM, October 17, 1989. You are in the vicinity of the earthquake's epicenter. Though there is little evidence here, slides and fissures occurred in more remote areas of the park." Being near the epicenter stirred an uneasy feeling in me, as though the earth below us were a monster waiting to open its jaws and swallow us whole.

"So where were you at the time of the earthquake?" I asked David. Dust powdered his face and sweat cut rivulets through it.

The earthquake had devastated most of downtown Santa Cruz. Everyone of remembering age knew where he or she had been. I'd been at home where the cupboards flew open and jars of spices shattered on the floor. The place reeked of vinegar. My ex-husband Chad had been roofing. The ladder had fallen and the two workers had clung to the chimney, probably not the smartest idea as many chimneys shook off their bricks and crumpled.

"You've asked me that before," David said. "Last time we were here."

A couple rode by us on a pair of blue Santa Cruz bikes. David enviously regarded their rides; I enviously regarded their youth.

I pushed David's arm to get his attention. He was now

staring at the young girl's butt. "If I remember right, you didn't answer."

"You don't want to know," he said.

I imagined this meant he'd been with another woman. I hated when men assumed I'd be jealous. I had faults, stubbornness and irritability near the top, but jealousy ranked low. Even as David watched the young woman's rump, I felt impatient more than jealous.

Whatever we both wanted to get off our chests, we needed to do it now. After this point, we would climb for four miles, taking us from near sea level to 1,500 feet. Another reason I disliked the ride. It embodied none of the Zen of picking a trail; it was a laborious uphill trudge. "What are you pissed off about?"

"Let's ride," he said.

"I don't think so," I replied. "Unless I ride home." I turned my bike for emphasis.

"I feel like I have to fucking beg to get any time with you."

"I work two jobs."

"Why?"

"I work one to support myself, and the other because it's what I want to do."

"Quit one."

"Which one?"

He unsnapped his helmet and took it off to cool his head. His dark hair was matted to his head, his dark eyes hidden by his wrap-around biking glasses. I didn't need to see them to know they would be pained and angry. "If you moved in with me, all your bills would be cut in half. Split the mortgage payment."

"I just bought out Chad; I don't know if I want to go back to owning half a house."

"Then keep your house and rent it," David argued, "and all those other bills, PG&E, PacBell, whatever, we could split. And when the faucet leaks, you won't have to hire a plumber, because you'll have me," he joked. "Mr. Fix It." He flashed me his big smile of white teeth, his first feature to charm me over a year ago.

I appreciated David's attempt to change the emotional current, but he was a more mercurial personality than I, quicker to anger, but also quicker to move beyond it. I still felt annoyed at his blithe suggestion that I quit one job; he seemed to have no grasp of my dilemma. Which one would I relinquish, my security blanket or my dream?

David put on his helmet and plucked his water bottle from his cage. "I suggest you hydrate, too."

"Yeah, well, before we begin the climb, maybe you could tell me what Leonard said."

"That's your reward for when we get to the top." He shoved his water bottle back into its rack and started up the hill.

I shifted down and down, all the way to my granny gear. My palms throbbed. I'd underestimated how much weight and effort went into the hands.

Sweat poured from my head. I'd left my thick auburn hair in the braid I wore to work, but if I'd had a scissors, I would have cut it off. It lay against my back like a hot, heavy boa constrictor. I spat dirt from my mouth and entertained nasty fantasies about David. Typical, macho jerk who always had to lead, so that I'd eat his dust. Let him ride ahead. Let him ride way ahead. I'd turn back. Let him get to Sand Point Overlook and wait for ten minutes, and then fifteen, wondering what had happened to me, growing anxious, fearing an accident, racing down the hill, alarmed now, kicking himself for not checking in . . . .

I stood up to pump, relieving my sore cheeks. I didn't like the bubble butt effect of bike shorts, but maybe it was time. On steeper sections, I traversed the trail as David had shown me. The flies, knowing I couldn't take my hands off the bars, came to suck the sweat off the backs of my knees.

At Sand Point Lookout, I found David resting on a log with the young bikers who'd passed us earlier. He beamed at me, proud of me for making it. I was proud of me, too. As I dismounted, my legs felt like Jell-O. I wheeled my Trek over to the group, plopped on to the log, and took off my helmet.

David patted me on a dusty leg. "Way to go." He turned to the youngins. "She's over forty. Can you believe that?"

They were real youngins, perhaps still in their teens, so they were unduly impressed. "Wow," the girl said, "my mom's forty. She could never do that."

I smiled, inspecting the blood seeping through the gauze on my palms.

The young couple stood and pulled their bikes from the ground. They were going to continue up the trail to an even steeper climb dubbed The Wall, which led into Demonstration Forest, a place for serious mountain bikers. David enviously watched them go. "You need a lighter bike," he announced.

"I just bought this one."

"I'll go in half."

"A lighter bike is not going to make me twenty again."

"You'll be amazed how much difference it makes."

We sat in silence for a moment, admiring the rolling vista of trees, the ocean a haze in the distance.

"I want my reward," I said.

"Okay, here's the deal. The first tidbit is that Harbor View Estates did not report any missing meds. They are required, by law, to file incident reports."

"I appreciate the dirt. I have to find a way to discourage my mom from going there."

I would let David believe I'd been inquiring about the facility on my mom's behalf, maybe let him feel a little guilty for assuming I was interested only in my case, not that he even knew what my case was. I had failed to tell David that Rusty Mills had hired me to look into his mother's will, not her death.

"You remember the Mildred Levine case?" he asked.

"The woman from Harbor View whose family is filing a civil suit. The woman with the deca . . . ."

"Decubitis." He reached down for the water bottles and handed me mine. "That family wants Leonard to testify. So he wanted to talk to the nurse . . . ."

"Nurse Motha?"

He nodded. "He went to the VNA to get her schedule, and discovered that's not her only place of employment. She's also on a registry and has worked at the skilled nursing facility where Mildred Levine died."

"That's it?" I asked impatiently. I'd toiled four miles up a mountain for this? "You told me yourself that these visiting nurses work all over. And you also told me how completely normal it is for people to die both in residential care facilities and nursing homes."

His information was interesting, but useless to me.

"True," David said. "I wouldn't think twice about this, but Leonard's gotten all excited by your suggestion of murder. He wants you to know that in spite of what he called a 'wild jigsaw schedule,' Nurse Motha was at the nursing home when Mildred Levine died. And, she was at Harbor View Estates when Gladys Mills died. She cared for both of them."

CHAPTER 25

The ride up Nisene Marks had taken us about an hour. The ride down took fifteen minutes. As we sped and bumped down the steep hill, I sat with my butt off the saddle and my hands gripping the handlebars. We stopped twice to let the rims of our tires cool so as not to burn out the brakes. My palms seared with pain.

After the exhilarating race down and a hot shower at home, it was easy to forget what I hated about the ride. I felt purified, sweated clean.

I inspected my hands. The person who had tackled me had knocked me flat and the shredded skin ran the length of my palm. Feeling pissed all over again, I slathered the wounds with Neosporin and rebandaged them. The attack seemed like a gross overreaction. All I had done was crash a party.

With my long, wet hair trickling on my tee-shirt, I grabbed a beer and padded out to my miniature patio. Lola was massaging herself by rolling on the bricks.

After the ride, David and I had parted on less than lovey-dovey terms. He had wanted me to spend the rest of the afternoon with him, preferably nestled in bed.

"I have to take a shower."

"Take one here."

The offer had been easy to refuse. His bathrooms looked like science experiments. *Mr. Fix It needs Mr. Clean.*

As I plopped down on the bricks with Lola, I thought of

Suzanne and how she'd ventured to Kuwait. She was much bolder than I, facing the scorching white sand of a foreign place for love. I wouldn't even face a little mold.

It was completely natural and fair for David to want our relationship to move to the next level. I couldn't keep putting him off.

I thought again of Suzanne. She had been excited to go with Hamad. To Kuwait! Hardly a place listed in travel brochures. That's what love would do to a person, so maybe I wasn't really in love.

I sipped my beer and reflected on how things that seemed hard and grinding at first, like the bike ride, could turn out to feel great. Rewarding.

Then I thought of all the work that would have to be done to David's house to make it habitable. I felt overwhelmed. "Besides, Lola likes it here. Don't you, Lola?"

If I passed over this opportunity with David, would I wind up as one of those dotty old women discovered dead with her twenty-four, half-feral cats roaming the house?

I rose restlessly and pinched spent blossoms from the cosmos in my tiny garden. Instead of feeling exhausted, I felt relaxed and energized. In terms of Rusty Mills' assignment, I should track down people who could attest to Gladys Mills' state of mind. I definitely wanted to talk to Chrissie, her assistant, heir to a house in Santa Cruz.

It might also be worthwhile to talk to Nurse Motha. As the only medical professional at Harbor View Estates, she'd be in a position to comment on Gladys's soundness of mind.

I didn't buy Leonard's farfetched idea that Nurse Motha could be connected to the deaths of Mildred Levine and Gladys Mills. I remembered, though, what Sherlock Holmes said about doctors: *When a doctor does go wrong, he is the first of criminals. He has nerve and he has knowledge.* The same, I supposed, would be true of a nurse run amok.

I shook my head. I pictured Nurse Motha as the angelic figure bent over my mom. *My mom.* I gulped. I needed to call her and see how she was doing.

I slid open the glass door and reentered my little queendom. I put the beer bottle in the recycle and the handful of spent flower blossoms in the trash. My next move had nothing to do with any of my thoughts. It had nothing to do with any logical pursuit of my case.

I pulled on socks and hightop sneakers. I brushed my teeth and used mouthwash to get rid of the telltale smell of beer. I threw on my black leather jacket, and stuffed money, driver's license and business cards in the pockets. Then I set off in my old, comfortable car: dilemmas at work, problems with David, and worries about my mother all swept conveniently to the back of my mind.

Stewart's Pharmacy was a miracle, a family run business that had escaped financial ruin in spite of the new Walgreens up the street. I could remember entering the store only once in my fifteen years in Santa Cruz for an emergency purchase of Tampax.

The store had survived by carving out a niche of personalized service to seniors. Stewart's featured an entire aisle of orthopedic devices, support hose, foot lifts and ankle braces, with a fine selection of canes at the end. Its choices for adult diapers were far superior to that for tampons.

Another key to the store's survival, I soon learned, was that Mrs. Stewart worked behind the counter and Mr. Stewart was the pharmacist.

Mrs. Stewart was a small, spry woman with gray hair cut in a pixie and soft cornflower blue eyes. Her name tag identified her as Bernadette. She bustled up to me and said, "Oooo, I know exactly what you need for that." She nodded at my bandaged palms, walked briskly down an aisle, and slid a product called Adaptic from its hanger.

I stared idly at the box.

"Non-adhering dressing," Mrs. Stewart explained. "They breathe."

I held the product respectfully in my hands. "Has the new Walgreens up the street had any effect on your business?" I asked.

She shrugged. "They're not really our competitors. We've tailored our business to seniors. We also supply Clayborne Surgical Center."

I'd never heard of the place.

"Outpatient surgery. Over by the hospital."

I still couldn't place it, so I made a lame comment about that sounding like a good account.

"It keeps us afloat." She smiled wanly, waiting for me to decide on the Adaptic or to state my business.

When I handed her my card and asked if I could talk to her about Jerry, her forehead wrinkled with concern.

"Is he in trouble? I'm his grandmother."

I shook my head.

"Excuse me." The woman went to the pharmacy, held a whispered conversation with the pharmacist, and returned with the man in tow. I used the opportunity to return the Adaptic to its spot.

Bernadette introduced him as "Jerry's grandfather," although his tag said: James Stewart, PharmD. Mr. Stewart was at least six foot four and had a lush head of chestnut colored hair that didn't seem quite real. Whether dyed or a toupee, I couldn't decide. He had a powerful handshake.

"Ms. Sabala wants to ask us some questions about Jerry," Mrs. Stewart said.

I was sure that she'd already explained this to her husband; this was her way of getting to the point.

I briefly explained my case. "I need to get hold of Chrissie to ask her what she might know about Gladys Mills, but I've been having trouble finding her." *When she's sober,* I added in my head.

"Oh, that girl," the grandmother said, waving one hand by her ear. "No wonder we have a private investigator here. Lucky it's not the cops."

Mr. Stewart cradled his chin and stroked his cheek with one finger. "If you ask me, Bernadette, Chrissie's a lot like our Alice."

Bernadette crossed her arms over her pink store smock. "Oh, not that tired Freudian theory again." She turned to me, but her eyes scanned the store. A middle aged woman was checking out the array of walkers. "James thinks Jerry is in love with a girl like his mother. Our daughter."

"How is Chrissie like your daughter, Mr. Stewart?"

"Please call me James."

I nodded. Bernadette Stewart edged away. She'd heard this all before and wasn't interested in hearing it again. Besides, a customer needed assistance. She didn't seem to care if Chrissie were in trouble, as long as Jerry wasn't.

"How is Chrissie like Jerry's mother?" I prompted.

"I've read that we pursue people like our parent of the opposite sex. What do you think of that idea?"

"I wouldn't know. My father deserted the family." I didn't usually share this information, but I wanted to get on with the conversation. "I don't have any way to judge." The question, though, stimulated my curiosity. *How did David compare to my father? The mysterious Geraldo Sabala.* On the surface, David was loyal, and that alone made him quite different.

"Alice was our baby girl," James Stewart mused. "We spoiled her."

Bernadette whipped her head around. "One of us spoiled her."

Mr. Stewart nodded sadly. "It's true. I spoiled her."

He lifted his white pharmacist's jacket and extracted a billfold from his back pocket. He flipped it open to a family photo.

People often visualize a PI as a tough guy grilling people with questions, but it's often more about listening. People yearned to be heard, to be understood. Confronted with a patient listener, they often poured out their hearts.

The photo showed the impossibly young parents seated with four preteen and teen boys standing behind them and a little girl of about seven pressed in close to her daddy with a thin arm draped around his neck. James already had a prominent bald spot, solving the mystery of his current hair, or rather hairpiece.

Alice had her mom's small build and large cornflower eyes with thick, thick lashes. I recognized the yellow plastic headband she used to push back her light brown hair. I'd had one just like it.

"My little girl."

"She'll be thirty-eight next week," the wife shot dryly over her shoulder.

"What happened to Alice?" I asked.

"Oh, she's around," James answered tiredly. "Probably in Santa Cruz, unless there's a Grateful Dead reunion somewhere."

"Jerry Garcia died last year," Bernadette said.

I remembered the time last August; the Grateful Dead followers were shocked that Jerry Garcia was dead, even though he was an overweight drug abuser with diabetes and a stressful schedule.

"There are concerts in his honor, and wherever they are, she's there. She's still a Dead Head," he pronounced.

Bernadette swooped in to add, "And a pothead." She'd left the customer avidly comparing two walkers, rolling first one, and then the other over the wooden floor. She opened the front door for an old woman hobbling up on a cane. "Hello, Mrs. Donaldson," she said cheerily.

Bernadette caught her husband's eye and subtly crooked her neck. After years of marriage, that was all it took.

"Let's go back to my office," James said.

The tiny office barely contained an old-fashioned, expansive oak desk heaped with papers. A small computer table and two file cabinets set at right angles to it. This office had been parsimoniously carved from floor space or had been an original office sacrificed bit by bit to an expanding pharmacy.

Mr. Stewart plopped into the hard chair that matched the oak desk. I gladly took the soft computer chair and rolled it back a bit so that we weren't Eskimo kissing.

Mr. Stewart laced his long hands on top his head as if to hold on his toupee.

"The drugs, of course, are one point of similarity between Chrissie and Alice," Mr. Stewart said. "Jerry spent his whole childhood taking care of his mom. I think it seems completely natural to him to be taking care of Chrissie."

"Taking care of her how?"

Mr. Stewart cleared his throat. Put his hands back in his lap. "Making sure she's okay," he said vaguely.

I wondered if that meant supplying Chrissie with drugs, and I wondered if Mr. Stewart knew it. As eager as he was to talk, Mr. Stewart struck me as a prudent man. He was a pharmacist—a careful, exacting person. He wasn't about to incriminate himself or his grandson. And Jerry knew his grandfather. I remembered his taunting, "Knock yourself out."

I did some quick math. Alice was thirty-eight, and Jerry looked in his young twenties. Alice must have gotten pregnant at an early age.

"Is Alice married?"

Mr. Stewart chuckled at this. "Alice has four children from four different men—one Hispanic, one black, one white, one Native American. Her own personal Rainbow Coalition."

He hadn't actually answered the question, but I sensed pain under his bewildered amusement and didn't press.

It was odd for me to think of this woman as my peer, only a little younger. What would it be like to have four children with no husband?

"Jerry is her oldest?"

He nodded. "A good boy. He got tired of touring the country

in one of those Volkswagen Vanagons. When he was ten, he told his mom that he wanted a good education and asked if he could come and live with us."

"So now Alice lives in a bus with three children?"

"No. Her daughter Phil moved in with her boyfriend's family last year. She's the one to worry about, not Jerry."

"Dark-haired girl?" I asked. The dots were connecting. Phil was the girl who had poured coffee on me. She was indeed one to worry about.

"Not by nature," James replied. He sat straight, and dispassionately continued his litany. "Vince Little Wolf lives with his dad. All Alice has now is Mickey. Alice named all her children for members of the Grateful Dead."

Alice wasn't the first woman who'd put all her excitement into the naming of her children as though they were simply new flavors of ice cream.

"Can I talk to Alice?" As Jerry and Phil's mom, I saw her as a potential link to Chrissie.

"If you can find her."

"You don't know where she is?"

"She parks wherever she can in Santa Cruz, often in the driveway of a friend. Other times she parks out by the Wrigley building. She's had year-or-so stints with boyfriends, but I don't think she's with anyone now. Her address is a post office box."

James Stewart delivered the information calmly, with an air of acceptance. Even though we proclaim acceptance as a virtue, I found the accompanying resignation sad.

"So no," he concluded, "I really couldn't tell you where she is."

"How often do you see her?"

He shrugged. "If she's in town and she's bored, she'll pop in the store on a regular basis, bring Bernadette some of her beaded jewelry, make me a Father's Day card. She hugs us and tells us that we're wonderful parents. Thanks us profusely for taking care of Jerry. Then she'll disappear and we might not see her for a year."

I nudged the conversation toward my real interest. "How are Chrissie and Alice alike?"

He smiled slightly and twined his long fingers. "They're both free spirits. Chrissie is a little older than Jerry. She swept him off his feet."

I translated this to mean that she'd turned him on to some hot sex.

"Alice has a way with men, too," he added.

"And both women are drug users?"

He bobbed his head philosophically. "But they're different in their attitudes."

"About drugs?"

"Yes. Alice enjoys altered states. Even when she was a little girl, she liked me to grab her by the arms and swing her in circles until she couldn't walk straight." Caught in the web of nostalgia, Mr. Stewart's arms flailed, his first real animation since we'd been seated in the cramped room. "She would stare at beach bon fires until she went into a trance-like state. I'm not saying I approve of her drug use," he said somberly, "but I understand it. It's consistent with her nature."

"And Chrissie?"

"She just likes to get messed up. By whatever means possible. It's not linked to music or misguided spirituality or anything. She's hell bent on self-destruction."

"Have you ever suspected Jerry of using drugs?"

The grandfather squirmed in his chair. "Oh, no. Jerry's a good boy. Almost too good. He's going to Cabrillo. I expect him to be a college graduate like my other grandkids. So far I have a commercial pilot, a nurse, a physics teacher, and a computer programmer," he listed proudly.

"Have you ever suspected Jerry of taking drugs?"

"Didn't you just ask me that?" Mr. Stewart sounded irritated now and his eyes strayed to the door.

I tried to roll back the computer chair so he'd have room to stretch his legs, but I was already against the wall. "I meant taking from the store."

"Why would he do that?"

"For Chrissie."

A patina of sweat collected on James Stewart's face.

"How does this have anything to do with the will you're investigating?"

"If Gladys Mills was murdered for her money, that could have a lot of bearing on her will."

James Stewart widened his eyes. "Murdered?"

I'd gone too far, but there was no going back. It wasn't my nature to go back, anyway. Chrissie and I had that in common; once our course was set, we rushed pall- mall down it. The bulls of Pamplona had nothing over us.

"Does Jerry need a lawyer?"

"Did I say anything about Jerry's involvement?"

The grandfather stood, his face flushed. "That's what you just insinuated. I think you should leave." He edged past me and held open the door of the office.

Bernadette materialized in the entrance. "Is everything okay?"

These two were magically connected. I stole by the woman. "Thanks for your time, Mrs. Stewart."

CHAPTER 26

From Soquel Drive I made my way up Ocean and then turned on Water Street to the dismal little office of Sloan's Investigative Services. I could understand why J.J. hung out at the bar. At least it had some life in it.

And it didn't smell any worse. The stench of burnt coffee permeated the office. I went to our back room and turned off the coffee maker, a Norelco Drip relic with a pot of tarry brew beneath it.

I sat in our squeaky desk chair and listened to fifteen phone messages, all for J.J. Some of them were two days old; J.J. was bad about erasing old messages, but he was also bad about checking in at the office. There was no way of knowing whether he'd heard these or not.

I headed down to the bar. J.J. occupied his usual spot at the end of the counter, drinking his supper. It looked like whiskey. J.J. did not limit his repertoire; he drank anything containing alcohol, except wine. Wine was for fruits.

A woman slouched on the stool beside him, studiously smoking, acting like she weren't interested in J.J. and that the woman standing beside him was nonexistent.

"Yo," J.J. shouted at the bartender. "Bring my partner a Guinness."

I didn't particularly like Guinness, and for all his conviviality, J.J. didn't offer to move to a table where I could sit. That was part of his code of ethics. Real drinkers perched at the bar.

"We have a message from our rich eccentric, among fifteen other messages," I chastised. The bartender plunked down a cold bottle. This was not the kind of place that offered glasses.

"I'm going to the office tonight," J.J. said.

I should have known. Even though he thought a real bar should be open for breakfast, J.J. usually didn't wake up until noon. He often went to bed about the time I was getting up to bake. I should have left the coffee burning.

"What did he want?" J.J. asked.

"I think he'd like us to rip out his neighbor's walls."

J.J. smiled crookedly over his too large, capped front teeth.

"He's convinced the contractor smuggled insulation into the new building during the night."

J.J. yawned. "Does he want more surveillance?" He looked hopefully at me.

"Don't even think about it," I said. "I'm busy on my Mills' case."

"How's that going?"

I held up my two taped palms.

"That looks exciting."

I sipped my beer and filled J.J. in on my investigation. In case Mr. Stewart decided to call my boss, I figured J.J. better know about my visit to Stewart's Pharmacy.

"Strong arm tactics, huh, Carol?" He smiled again. It did nothing to lighten his smashed face.

I defended myself. "Gladys Mills might have been murdered."

"Maybe," J.J. said and ordered another drink. "But you haven't been hired to investigate that."

"No one cares this woman may have been killed," I whined. "Not even her son."

"Ours is not to wonder why," he said evenly.

Herein lay the problem with official investigating. I'd had more freedom as a rogue snoop. Professionals worked for clients.

We did what the client wanted, even if it meant sitting for hours with binoculars trained on his neighbor's new construction.

"It sounds like this guy, Rusty, wants you to question the girl. I don't understand that. She's no expert on Gladys Mills' state of mind. It would make a lot more sense to talk to the nurse. But, if that's what he wants . . . . His voice trailed off and he gulped his drink. "It's like the sign in the toilet: We aim to please. You aim, too, please."

CHAPTER 27

When I got home, I was ravenous. I'd eaten a free lunch at work, but had since climbed a mountain on a bike, and put in hours at my second job with nary a bite to eat. Her Royal Highness Lola rubbed against my leg, but I didn't even stop to scratch her ears.

Instead, I heated oil in a frying pan and sautéed the remains of a shriveled yellow onion while I mixed two eggs with a bit of milk and water. I found a cube of cheddar cheese, cut off the mold and grated it. I toasted two slices of stale bread while I scrambled the eggs. Saliva pooled in my mouth.

As I dug into my meal, Lola jumped into my lap. No soufflé at Archibald's had ever tasted finer. Lola gingerly licked the last crumb of egg from my fingertip.

I checked my messages and was astonished to find I had three. The first one was from David. He told me that he'd had fun on the ride and thanked me for being a good sport. He wished me sweet dreams. He did not try to wheedle me to spend the night. So even though apparently all was forgiven, I felt disappointed.

I could call him. Invite myself. I pondered this, the fear of rejection growing. *How did men do it?*

As I tried to work up the courage, I listened to the next message. It was from Dominican Hospital. My mom had been admitted.

In a panic, I grabbed my leather jacket and shot out the door.

Visiting hours lasted until eight thirty. I found out her room number at information and galloped up the stairs and down the polished hallway. My mother's eyes were closed. Against the white pillow, her face looked ashen.

"Mom," I said softly.

She didn't stir. She was on her back with her arms outside the thin blanket and crossed over her stomach in the coffin pose. I couldn't help myself. I pressed my thumb against her wrist.

"What are you doing?" she croaked. Her eyelids fluttered open.

"God, Mom? What happened?" I guiltily retracted my hand.

"I'm not dead," she said crabbily. "Yet."

"I'm glad." My eyes misted. I sat in the chair by her bed. Her eyes drifted shut. I felt like shaking her. How dare she go back to sleep before giving me an explanation?

Why hadn't she called me?

I felt enormously relieved, but pissed. What would I do if my mom died? Did she, like Gladys, have a will that made her wishes known? Where did she keep it?

My heart raced. A big stopper had been plunged into my throat; I couldn't swallow. I couldn't breathe. I massaged my throat to coax it to relax.

I pictured my mom in a grave. *Alone.* Myself abandoned. My family all gone. No husband. Suzanne, my best friend, half way around the world in Kuwait. I'd always imagined that I was independent, that I didn't mind being alone. Now I realized that I'd never been alone.

"Are you the daughter?"

Startled, I turned to the door. A heavy-set, Afro-American nurse stood there. Her dark eyes looked kind, but her demeanor warned not to try any sort of monkey business. "Yes, I'm Carol Sabala."

The nurse bustled forward, shook my hand and introduced herself. She motioned for me to follow her into the hallway. There she gave me the whole story.

Someone from the Hinds House where my mother lived had driven her to the hospital that afternoon. My mom complained of a horrible stomachache. The doctor had discovered a tumor in her stomach the size of a grapefruit. The tumor needed to be removed, but my mom's heart was weak. Before they could operate to remove the tumor, they'd have to do heart surgery. Without improved blood pressure, my mom would not be able to survive the second surgery which was necessary because the tumor was pressing on her bowels.

Jesus, I thought, *no wonder she'd been feeling a little poky lately. No wonder she'd needed a little roughage.*

Then I felt angry again. My mom hadn't said anything about her stomach to Dr. Jellinek.

"Do you ever have visiting nurses work here?"

The black nurse frowned at me. "You mean like from the VNA?"

I nodded.

She shook her head, perplexed. "They might work with our out patients, but not here in the hospital."

I had resisted the idea of Nurse Motha as a killer, but I was eased, knowing that she wouldn't be around my mother.

After the nurse left, I used the phone in my mom's room to call work. Fortunately, tomorrow was my day off, but citing a family emergency, I left a message that I would not be in Tuesday. After our discussion this morning, Eldon would explode like an overfilled cream puff.

CHAPTER 28

No one rousted me from the room at eight-thirty. I woke in the middle of the night, disoriented and slouched in an uncomfortable hospital chair. My chin had been lolling on my chest and I could barely straighten my stiff neck. My bruised hands hurt and my legs ached from the bike ride up Nisene Marks.

Light from the hallway partially illuminated the room and my mom looked ghostly. I wouldn't have been surprised to see her lift from the bed and float about the room, seeking her escape from this world.

I couldn't help myself. I pressed my thumb to her wrist.

Her eyelids fluttered.

What was this? You'd think my thumb were a cattle prod.

"Don't they have machines to tell you if I'm dead," my mom grumbled.

I patted her hand. "You're going to be fine."

"Don't give me that malarkey." She sounded like she wanted to argue, but was too exhausted to continue.

"Why didn't you call me, Mom?"

"I did," she croaked. "Twice."

I wanted to grill her with questions, but instead said, "Shhhh. You need to rest, Mom."

"It's silly to say you have an emergency on a message machine, don't you think?"

"You're right, Mom."

She fell back to sleep with a satisfied smile on her face.

Reassured by the brief conversation, I went home, called my mom's only remaining sibling, Teddy, to tell him the news and then climbed into bed. I'd once used an exquisite star quilt as a spread, but it had been shot and splattered with blood. My only remaining blanket was a crazy quilt with puckered corners that my mother had made for me, a much less fine work as far as craftsmanship went.

I pulled the heavy blanket around my shoulders and stroked the forest green and dusty rose swatches of soft flannels and velveteen. Whenever I had those philosophical ponderings of what would I rescue if my house caught on fire, Lola came first, then the blanket.

Lola jumped on to the bed and settled herself in the curl of my legs. Her life and warmth reassured me.

I didn't wake up until nine the next morning. It was as disquieting as waking up in the hospital chair. I bounded out of bed for no reason, eliciting a squeak of protest from Lola.

Visiting hours at the hospital didn't start until eleven, and even though they hadn't shooed me out the night before, I didn't have a good feeling about being admitted early.

After showering, I poured a cup of black coffee over some Cheerios and ate standing up. Part of a nutritious breakfast.

I poured the rest of the coffee to go. The only problem with my old Ghia, besides lack of air bags, was the lack of a mug holder. I drove with the thermos mug between my legs. Needing to kill time until visiting hours at the hospital, I headed to Harbor View Estates. I popped in a tape of the B-52's and listened to the band belt out, *"You're living in your own private Idaho."* Yes, indeed, I did feel like an underground potato, but between the caffeine and music, I expected to unearth myself at any moment.

Nurse Motha was the logical person to question about Gladys Mills and if I remembered correctly, she'd been there on my mom's first visit, a Monday, so presumably Nurse Motha would be making her rounds today.

To avoid the reception area and the stiff Katherine O'Conner, I used an entrance into a residential wing. The place was very quiet at ten o'clock in the morning. I padded the entire length of Gladys's former wing without spotting a soul.

At the end of the hall the wing formed a T-intersection with two other residential wings. At the intersection was a lounge area complete with a big screen television. Two women rested on one of the couches. They didn't seem to be conversing. I wondered if they were watching the blank screen. I recognized Harriet McGruder, the ice cream eater from the cafeteria.

"Hello, Harriet," I greeted her.

She peered at me.

"Carol Sabala," I prompted. "Gladys Mills' acquaintance."

Harriet nodded, but I was unconvinced that she had her marbles today.

"Have you seen Nurse Motha?"

"The sadist?"

"Why do you say that?"

She crooked her frail, liver-spotted finger. I drew closer.

"Lift up my blouse."

I hesitated.

"You're an investigator, aren't you?"

"Yesss."

"Don't worry. I won't cry sexual harassment."

She seized my hand. Bony, unreal fingers gripped me. I was in the clutches of E.T. "Just the back."

I looked at the other woman. She gazed at the blank screen with rapt attention.

Perhaps Harriet McGruder wanted to hire me. I gingerly hoisted the tail of the woman's white blouse. She wore an undershirt.

"You'll have to do better than that," Harriet complained. She released my hand and reached around to tug ineffectually at her shirt.

"What am I looking for?"

"The bruise."

"Nurse Motha bruised you?"

"Hit me," the old woman said.

I tugged the undershirt from the waist of her slacks and worked the two shirts up her back. The skin hung loosely. Not even a diet of ice cream could maintain the plumpness of youth. I checked the bandages on my palms. I didn't want to get blood on her white clothing.

The daisy sized bruise, a sickly yellow green, blossomed over her substantial bra strap.

I lowered her undershirt and blouse. "Nurse Motha hit you for no reason?"

The woman nodded and kept nodding like a stuffed animal with a spring loaded head. She turned to her friend. "What's on television?"

The woman gave me no clue how to interpret the last couple of minutes. I half expected her to ask me again if I were going to work at Harbor View.

"You'll find the sadist in room 806," Harriet said succinctly.

To my good fortune, I caught up with Nurse Motha as she was leaving the room. I halted at the sight of the hypodermic in her left hand.

Nurse Motha recognized me at once. "How's your mother doing?" she asked pleasantly.

The question pierced me like the arrow shot into Achilles' heel. One moment I was a fierce warrior, charged with indignation, the next I was mortally wounded. Warily watching the needle, I relayed what had happened with my mom since the day of Gladys's death.

The nurse stepped toward me and I stepped back.

She glanced at the hypodermic. "Do you have a fear of needles?" She patted my shoulder with her free hand.

I had a fear of needles wielded by her.

"I don't blame you. Needle pricks are the most dangerous part of my job. But don't worry. I use the retractable kind."

Her left arm swished into the air. I winced. She held up the plunger to show me I'd imagined the needle. This was the reason eye witnesses were so unreliable. We saw what we expected instead of what really existed.

I took a deep breath. "My mom and I brought you some sunflowers the day Gladys died," I said. "But with everything that happened, we never did thank you for your help."

"Your mother is in good hands at Dominican," the nurse assured me. She paused. "Have you had any luck tracking down Chrissie?" She smiled at my surprise. "Gossip is the life's blood of places like this."

"Why would you care if I found her or not? From what I heard, your relationship wasn't any love fest."

Another small smile flickered wanly across the cherub face. "Chrissie was sullen to everyone. I didn't take it personally. I have some stuff to return to her."

I pounced. "What kind of stuff?"

"A few personal effects from Gladys's room." The woman ruffled like an animal on alert. "A sweater. Make up."

Why did she want to return them to Chrissie? If Chrissie cared about the things, she could come by HVE to retrieve them.

"Where are these items?" I shot.

The nurse compressed her lips. "I'm not sure."

"I understand Gladys was one of your clients," I said, trying to sound casual.

Nurse Motha shifted on to one hip and stared at me. "Yes, her son Rusty contracted with the VNA to have her checked once a week."

"Do you remember that on the day she died, Gladys didn't have any oxygen?"

The nurse flushed. "That's impossible. I checked her tank

that very day."

"There wasn't any tank."

"You must be mistaken," she said crisply.

I was not mistaken. My mom had called for the tank and it had not been there.

An awkward silence grew between us. "Gladys was quite a character," I prompted, trying for perky.

The nurse's forehead furrowed and her eyes became distracted.

"My mom and Gladys were becoming friends," I said, "but I couldn't tell if Gladys was all there."

The nurse eyed me peculiarly. "Oh, she was all there. A little insane with the smoking, but all there." She glanced down the hallway. "Were you by chance just talking to Harriet McGruder?"

"Yes."

The nurse rolled her eyes and shifted her hefty body. "Is that why you're grilling me? Did she tell you that I hit her?"

"She had me look at the bruise."

She heaved a sigh. "And people wonder why it's hard to get good care for the elderly."

"What happened?"

"She was choking on a turkey slice. Before resorting to the Heimlich maneuver, I gave her a nice, firm clap on the back and launched the turkey half way across the table."

"The woman must bruise easily."

"We filed an incident report. But if you want to believe Harriet, I was trying to kill her."

By noon I was back home. At the hospital, they'd been prepping my mom for her surgery and my visit had been brief.

Thinking about the bruise on Harriet McGruder's back, I restlessly paced my little house. David would not like what I decided to do. He would not like it at all. But I wasn't just his girlfriend; I was also a private citizen, and as such, I had every right in the world to do what I was about to do. I looked up the phone number for Community Care Licensing. The office was in San Jose. As I punched in the number, I saw the red three and remembered that I had an unchecked message.

The secretary transferred me to Leonard's office. "I hope this call is to tell me David has only a week more to live," Leonard joked. "Tell me you're sitting in your hot tub."

"I'm sorry to disappoint you, Leonard, but I don't have a hot tub. I don't even have a bathtub."

"The shower will do."

"I don't think a phone call in a shower would work very well."

"Why are women like that?" Leonard complained. "Dampening perfectly good fantasies with reality?"

"I'm not going to dampen your fantasies; I'm going to rain on them. I called to find out about Gladys Mills' oxygen tank."

Silence greeted me. I'd doused any enthusiasm he'd felt for this call. "I can only discuss things that are a matter of public record."

"I don't want you to discuss anything, simply confirm my information."

"Shoot."

"Gladys Mills should have had a full oxygen tank in her room, but there was none."

"Affirmative. There's a receipt that shows the oxygen was received."

"So either Nurse Motha is lying about putting it in her room, or someone removed it."

"That would seem to be true."

"Someone didn't want Gladys to be resuscitated. The person not only removed the oxygen tank, but also flipped the emergency call cord over the shower stall rod."

There was thoughtful silence on the other end of the line.

"The emergency cord doesn't mean anything, Carol," he said regretfully. "It could just be sloppy housekeeping. The woman had another cord by her bed." I could hear Leonard drumming on his desk. "Listen, Carol, those things don't work like fire alarms, anyway. They get yanked a hundred times a day—an old lady drops her fork and can't pick it up, or Mr. So and So gets stuck in his pajamas. People respond eventually, but they don't rush to the room like it's on fire."

I knew everything Leonard told me was true, and yet it seemed jaded. He had been doing his job a long time and had seen enough so that there was an explanation for everything. Nothing alarmed him. That was the danger of experience.

"That girl who went running down the hall for the nurse did the right thing," he said.

So Chrissie had been a hero while I had been in the room stupidly pulling a useless string.

"How about the oxygen tank? Have you told Rusty Mills about that?"

"God, Carol, the guy's trying to see if there are grounds for a wrongful death suit. He calls at least twice a day. We've been over every minute detail about twenty or forty times."

Any excitement Leonard had possessed about a possible link between Gladys's and Mildred Levine's deaths had dissipated. "The guy is driving me nuts."

As annoying as Rusty was, he might have been calling for good reason. For all her angelic appearance and competence, Nurse Motha had easy means to kill Gladys Mills. "Did the facility file an incident report regarding Nurse Motha and Harriet McGruder?"

"Geez, Carol, I don't know. I receive a dozen incident reports every day, so and so fell out of his chair, so and so burned his finger. I'll have to look."

After I completed the call with Leonard, my personal state bureaucrat, I listened to my third message.

It was from Rusty Mills. The guy had my home phone number, too. But then I remembered leaving it, clearly written and labeled with my name, beside his mother's chair.

Rusty Mills wanted to know what I'd learned about Chrissie. *Chrissie, Chrissie, Chrissie. What was with this guy and Chrissie?* I empathized with Leonard.

Rusty was my client and an impatient one. I should have picked up the phone and called him right then. Even if I didn't have anything on Chrissie, I had information that might advance a civil case. But, instead of calling, I puttered about the house, rationalizing that I didn't have anything to report. In the next hour, that was all about to change.

CHAPTER 29

I restlessly paced my house, waiting for a reasonable amount of time to elapse before checking back at the hospital. I put grape jelly in a container and sat it on the ledge of my back fence to see if I could attract the oriole from my palm tree. The male oriole's brilliant yellow was worth seeing up close and personal.

I did other important things like balancing my check book and cleaning behind the refrigerator. When the phone rang, it could have been a nuclear explosion. Adrenaline shot from the arches of my feet through my scalp. If I had short hair, it would have stood on end.

The hospital, I thought. *That could only be bad news.*

My second thought was Rusty.

A soft, tentative female voice asked, "Carol Sabala?"

My heart sank. This was a sweet voice to deliver bad news.

"This is Bernadette Stewart. We met yesterday."

I heaved a sigh of relief.

"My husband does not agree with me calling you," she prefaced. "I need to know if what I tell you can be held in confidence?"

"I'm not the police," I explained. On the other hand, she was not my client. If she told me something I should report to Rusty Mills, I would.

Bernadette Stewart proceeded. "I told my husband that we are *not* making the same mistake with Jerry that we made with

Alice, always coddling and protecting her. All she learned from us was if she attached herself like a barnacle to some kind-hearted man like James, or in her case *men*, she could take a free ride through life."

"I'm glad you've called," I said.

"We have been missing bottles of pills—Vicodin, Demerol, Percodan. Not all at once, but one here and one there. As much as we wanted to believe some street person took those prescriptions, the fact is they are kept in the pharmacy."

"So you think Jerry was taking them?"

"Not for himself. For his girlfriend."

"Did you confront him?"

"James would rather believe he's becoming senile than Jerry has been stealing from us. As for me, I told Jerry to stop seeing Chrissie. I said she was a bad influence."

"How did he respond?"

"He moved out and told us we should fire him. When people are in love, criticizing their boyfriend or girlfriend only alienates them."

"If you don't want to enable Jerry, maybe you should fire him."

"We thought about it, but James would rather have him steal from us than from another employer."

For all his education and success in business, James had all the classic characteristics of an enabler, or to avoid pop psychology lingo—a sucker. He probably rationalized that Jerry didn't take that much.

"Has anything else unusual happened at the store? Any missing syringes, that kind of thing?"

"Is Chrissie doing needle drugs?" she asked in alarm, as though this made the matter worse.

"I don't know." I felt like reminding her that people died from prescription drugs, too. Judy Garland, Elvis Presley, Marilyn Monroe, for examples. I bit my tongue. Ninety percent of wisdom lies in tongue biting.

"No," Bernadette Stewart continued thoughtfully, "nothing like that. But James did receive a weird billing. Just today, as a matter of fact. For something he can't remember ordering. Some mivacurium chloride. We assumed it was a billing error. It isn't anything a pill popper would be interested in."

CHAPTER 30

The Internet was an amazing thing. Within the hour, I knew everything I wanted about mivacurium chloride. A clear liquid that came in an ampule, mivacurium chloride served to paralyze muscles and was used to facilitate tracheal intubation.

In the wild jungles of the Amazon, the Orinocos had used its relative curare to render their prey and enemies helpless. As Bernadette Stewart had noted, the drug wouldn't hold much interest for a pill popper. But it would for a murderer.

The death would have been horrible. Gladys would have been wide awake and slowly suffocating.

Anger surged through me. I pictured my mother instead of Gladys. An incapacitated elder. Such an easy victim. Blood pounded against my skull.

Mivacurium chloride peaked in a few minutes and could be eliminated through the kidneys in twenty, so when the bladder released in death, there went the evidence. Provided enough curiosity were aroused to look for evidence.

Fortunately, one side effect of mivacurium chloride could be erythema and, in Gladys's case, the redness had called attention to the needle prick.

Rusty had been right all along. I needed to talk to Chrissie. If she'd murdered Gladys to get her greedy little hands on a house, that might invalidate her claim on the will. All of this investigation could be legitimately billed. J.J. would be ecstatic.

I called the house of Michael and Melanie Locatelli. Chrissie had not been home. "She usually checks in by now," Melanie said. "She still has a semblance of fashion and likes to change her clothes."

"Do you think she's at Jerry's?"

I could hear the woman shrug. "Maybe. But Jerry works. Chrissie is not the type to hang out in an empty apartment."

I wanted to slap her. If she gave just the littlest shit about Chrissie, maybe the girl wouldn't be a psycho pill-popping murderer.

Except Chrissie wasn't a girl. She was an adult. And Melanie had arrived too late on the scene to have much effect on her. If I wanted to blame a parent, I should focus on the smooth-talking Michael Locatelli or the absent mother.

But how much did parents have to do with their kids' choices anyway? You had straight arrow parents like James and Bernadette who produced children like Alice, and then Alice turned out a kid like Jerry, who except for his involvement with Chrissie, seemed more like his grandparents.

One of my mom's maxims was that parents blamed themselves too much for their kids' failures and took too much credit for their successes.

Guilt nudged my shoulder. I hadn't thought of my mom in over an hour. As she underwent her heart surgery, I should be holding her in my thoughts. Guilt shoved me roughly, two hands to the back. *This is Santa Cruz. You should be at the hospital, as close as possible, sending your mom positive energy.* Guilt tried to pass herself off as a delicate fairy, but she was a mean little bitch with a black leather whip.

I checked the clock on my computer. I didn't expect my mom to be out of surgery for another hour.

I wondered if my mom had been presented with the choice of which child to save, like Sophie in Sophie's Choice, if she would have rescued Donald rather than me. Even though my mom had never openly acknowledged Donald's sexuality, they'd been much more comfortable together than my mom and I were. Donald had never felt the need to push his gayness at her. "Oh, she knows," he said. When I tried to get my mother to talk about Donald's orientation, she said, "Some things are private." She and Donald accepted each other without any need to hash things out.

I was the monkey in the wrench, the thorn in the side. I hit the side of my head to knock the clichés out my ear, but all I did was remind myself that my palms hurt.

I stretched and got up from my desk. In my hunt for Chrissie, the downtown mall seemed like the best place to start, but maybe Jerry could focus my search a bit. It was one thing for him to act tough when sending me to interrogate his doting grandparents; he might act differently when confronted with a possible accessory to murder charge.

Remembering Chrissie's pal with the shaved head and cold eyes and the way I'd been flung to the asphalt, I lifted the Colt from my locked desk drawer. With its two-inch barrel it was easy to conceal. Usually I liked to investigate unencumbered by a purse, but today my shoulder bag was going with me.

Ten minutes later I pulled into the parking lot of Stewart's Pharmacy. I parked off to the side so Jerry and his grandmother wouldn't see me crossing the lot. In my jeans, scooped neck pink tee, and high top Converse, I looked like a well-preserved middle-aged woman dropping by to pick up some Viagra for her boyfriend. I'd tied my long thick hair into a loose braid down my back. I didn't want it getting in the way should I need to wrestle some punk to the floor.

I approached a door that ensured the clerk's back would be to me. Weighted with the revolver, my purse beat a rhythm against my hip.

Jerry stood behind the cash register, inserting a new roll of paper, his head bent. The nape of his neck looked thin and milky, like a child's. His white dress shirt hung off his shoulders as though there were nothing in the men's section that fit his slight build. He didn't have the heft of a man yet. I wondered how old he was.

He looked up, startled, when I entered. His eyes flicked to the pharmacy. Grandpa was there. His grandmother was not around.

"Did you come to talk to my grandparents?" he asked, trying for the bravado of the night before last.

"I talked to them yesterday."

Jerry paled.

"And your grandmother called me today."

Jerry tried to feed the register tape through the slot in the top, but his hands were shaking. A customer approached the counter with a hand basket of items. I reached across the Formica, threaded the tape for Jerry, and snapped the top back on the register.

He greeted the patron with all the good cheer of a death row inmate.

The customer didn't care. She was busy perusing an amazing array of plastic. She had at least ten cards in the side of her wallet, cards for Penny's and Sears and Shell gas. Did the woman bite at every special offer? Did she use all these cards? The paper work would be mind boggling.

When the customer had finally decided on her Bank of America Visa and Jerry had sent her out the door with her choice of plastic bags, he said, "What did Grammy tell you?"

Grammy. Jesus. He was still a boy.

"She told me about some bottles of missing pills."

He didn't say anything, but his head nodded involuntarily, acknowledging the deed.

"For Chrissie, I assume."

Without his ring of cohorts, he had no toughness to him at all. He was a mightily handsome boy with thick, damp lashes over jade green eyes.

"Where did you meet Chrissie?" I asked.

"Here," he croaked.

A good-looking guy in a drug store. Like a vampire, Chrissie must have homed in on that tender neck. But if, as James Stewart suggested, Chrissie was like Jerry's mom, Jerry might be fulfilling some wishes of his own. By supplying Chrissie's self-destructive habit, Jerry could be indulging in symbolic matricide.

Call me Carol Freud.

"Your grandmother also told me about an order for mivacurium chloride."

The kid was smart enough not to say anything. He looked toward the pharmacy. Good old grandpa. His life raft.

"Yeah, you should tell grandpa to hire you that lawyer." I waited a beat. "I just want to know where I can find Chrissie."

He didn't answer. Love had struck him all the way dumb.

CHAPTER 31

The doctor came out to talk to me. This couldn't be a good sign. My heart thudded.

He was a tall, lean man like James Stewart, but minus the toupee. He carried a clipboard and looked somber, but at least his surgery greens weren't splattered with blood.

"The surgery went fine," he reported. "You can sit with your mom, but she won't be in any condition to converse."

My mom didn't converse on her best of days.

"She'll recuperate here for a few days, but you need to think about her outpatient care. When she leaves here, she'll hardly be in any position to jump up and make meals. She may have difficulty even getting back and forth to the bathroom. She'll need several weeks to mend before we attempt the other surgery."

He dismissed me to my mother's room. What was I going to do? I had to work. I couldn't care for my mother.

I slipped into my mother's room and sat in the dim silence. I watched the IV drip.

When I caught myself an hour later pointlessly reading an article in the June issue of People about Emerson, Lake and Palmer, a group I hadn't cared about even in their Seventies glory, I knew I had to do something different, as utterly fascinating as it was to see how a shirtless, long-haired guy in a beaded choker turned into a trench coat wearing middle aged man with a widow's peak.

I didn't completely trust that anyone at Archibald's had

checked the messages, so I called to make sure they knew I wouldn't be in the next day. I had the misfortune to reach Eldon in person. I explained the family emergency to him.

Eldon expressed his sympathy. He was a correct, polite person. "This is precisely why we need two bakers," he finished, unable to help himself. "Your mother could need help for weeks. I'm going to start the interviewing process, Carol."

Eldon could be tediously deliberate about making decisions, trying to gather everyone's opinion and to estimate the cost down to the pennies, but once he made up his mind, there was no use arguing with him. He took on the full weight of kitchen management, but he also relished the power. The kitchen of Archibald's was his life.

As I walked to my Ghia, my life bombarded me—my full-time baking job in jeopardy, my mother looking like cold mashed potatoes, my relationship with David in turmoil, and a client who demanded I track down an elusive street punk. Once I settled into the cracked seat, molded to my body, the feeling evaporated. I had everything I needed right here—driver's license, money, clothes, shelter. Life didn't have to be complicated. Maybe Jerry's mom had the right idea. If only Lola liked to ride in my car.

David's house was on the other side of the freeway and in less than five minutes I was pulling into his driveway. I'd never been the kind of girl who liked floral prints and puffy pink pillows, but this ranch style house should have a sign on it that said: Boys Club. Everything from the brown on brown paint to the pounding rock music to the miter saw on the porch covered with sawdust screamed bachelor pad. Before I reached the door, David padded out barefoot carrying a drill.

"Am I in trouble?" he asked.

"Why do you ask?" I hated that he was barefoot while I had shoes on. I didn't like being taller.

"You're here. You must be investigating a case. I'm sure you didn't come to visit any more than you called Leonard to chat."

Uh oh. I was in double trouble. It wasn't just that I'd called Leonard; I'd been neglectful. As a person who took a lively interest in his friends' lives, David expected the same treatment. He was busy building frames, probably for Open Studios in October, the biggest event of the year for his photography. I didn't even know the dates. I made a flabby effort. "What photograph are you going to put in the Open Studios' show?"

"Don't change the subject. Did you think Leonard wouldn't tell me?"

"I didn't consider it one way or the other."

"I don't want you using my friends, Carol."

"I wasn't using him."

"Oh, that was a social call?"

"Leonard's a big boy. If he doesn't want to supply information, he can say no."

David kneeled down, sat the drill on the porch, and held together two mitered pieces of frame. "Perfect," he muttered.

"Why are you making a frame?" I asked. Usually he used pre-fab, metal frames.

"I was thinking some of my shots where the subjects are in nature might look better with wood."

"Are you going to stain the wood?"

"What do you think?"

"It's a lot of work."

He arranged all four edges of the frame together on the porch and stared at them critically.

"I came to ask for a favor."

He sat back on his haunches. "I hope it has something to do with being naked and sweaty."

"I wish."

He wiped his hands on his shorts, ready to abandon his project. "I can make wishes come true."

I smiled. David was easy to anger, but he also let go of his anger easily, while I clutched anger like a flotation device, the only thing between me and the murky depths.

I sat on the porch step and he joined me. I told him about my mom. "I think she'll need residential care sooner rather than later, one with assisted living for now, but where she can convert to independent living when she's recovered. Some place where they don't serve Tang."

"I'll ask Leonard what he recommends." The dark brown eyes regarded me hopefully. "What are you up to now?"

"I'm trying to track down a girl."

"Could I hire you to do that for me?"

"Sure."

"I'd like her to be about five foot eight, athletic, with wild thick hair. Intelligent. Sense of humor. Scraped hands."

I smiled. The second time in five minutes. That was why I liked this guy.

On the other hand, David was as prickly and sticky as a cocklebur, and it had taken painful prying to leave him at his house as I continued my search for Chrissie Locatelli.

I banged on the splintered door and then peered in the windows of Jerry's apartment, but deserted houses felt empty, regardless of the tricks people tried with lights and radios on timers. I drove to the downtown mall.

From the clock tower end, I began walking down the east side of Pacific Avenue. Neither Chrissie nor her buddies loitered outside the Coffee Roasting Company. I did a quick tour of the interior and continued my jaunt all the way to Laurel, ducking in and out of likely joints. The aching muscles in my legs began to stretch and loosen. I headed up the other side of Pacific.

I never found Chrissie, but her scrawny, dark-haired friend occupied a prime spot on the sidewalk in front of Starbuck's, a collection bowl at the toe of her tennis shoes. They were the cheap white Woolworth's kind that she'd decorated with markers and wore without laces.

"What's up?" I asked. She had a pathetic fifty-seven cents in her bowl.

"The sky."

"I'm looking for Chrissie, Phil."

She smirked that I knew her name. "Did you bring any money this time?" She leaned into a black backpack propped against a light pole.

I reached in my purse, tweezered out a crisp twenty, squatted down, and played it like an accordion in front of her face. My thighs reminded me of the climb up Nisene Marks.

"I see the stains came out of your pants."

Jesus. This girl begged you to hit her. Life in a Vanagon must not have suited her.

I stood. "This is a different pair."

"You actually have two pairs like that?"

"Three." *Since when had 50l Levi's gone out of fashion?* I stuffed the twenty in my purse. *Where did she get the nerve? The cheek? The gall?* She wore the same mini-skirt and mini-shirt she'd been wearing two days ago, grungy from sitting on the sidewalk. Her knees were drawn up, so anyone who cared could see her pink panties. She'd changed into more comfortable shoes. Maybe she'd sold the boots, a purchase from better days when she had a job flipping burgers.

The dark eyes squinted up at me. "Can I still get the money if I don't know where Chrissie is?"

"Maybe." My thighs protested as I returned to a squat. "If you have a good lead."

Phil bit her black lips. "Do you have a cigarette?"

I shook my head. Phil looked up at the passersby. "Cigarette?" she asked. "Cigarette?"

I felt like screaming, "Would someone please give her a fucking cigarette!"

"Chrissie's scared."

She should be, I thought.

"Cigarette?"

"Get a job."

"Fuck you." Phil's voice was so toneless, she could have been saying thank you. "Chrissie thinks that someone is after her."

"I'm looking for her."

"Somebody who wants to kill her."

"Well, I don't want to kill her," I reassured the girl.

Phil giggled. "She's not afraid of you." She fiddled with her nose ring. The pale skin around it was red.

Her statement pissed me off more than the remarks about my clothes. *Why wasn't the little punk afraid of me?* Did I give off some wimpy vibe? I was four inches taller than Chrissie and carried at least twenty more pounds of muscle mass. I could kick her butt from here to kingdom come.

Phil laughed harder.

"What?" I asked angrily.

"You have a funny face."

"Thanks."

"I don't mean it like that. Your face is like watching television. You can see everything you're thinking and feeling."

Ah so. The girl meant revealing face; she simply had a limited vocabulary.

"Cigarette?"

A guy who looked like a street urchin himself tossed one in her bowl.

"Thanks, dude."

He flipped her a peace sign. "Get a job."

"Fuck you, bitch." Phil twisted around to her pack, dug a Bic lighter from a pocket, and lit up. She sucked hard at the cigarette. "Fuckin' cigarette light," she muttered. "Five finger discount, no doubt. No wonder he's giving them away."

"Do you think someone is after Chrissie?" I asked.

"No. It's one of those little dramas Chrissie makes up to keep my brother scurrying like a hamster, so he won't notice she's a pill addict loser." Phil laughed. "You think that's harsh coming from a loser like me."

I had to give the girl credit. She might not have read much else, but she could certainly read my face.

"I'm an expert on losers." She laughed mirthlessly.

I took the now crumpled twenty from my purse. "So where is she?"

"With my mom." She reached for the money. "Mommy Dearest will take in anyone. That sounds all nice, but it sucks if you're her kid with about two cubic feet of space to live in."

I yanked the Jackson back from her nicotine-starved fingers. "Where's your mom?"

"Who knows? That's the beauty of hiding out with her."

CHAPTER 32

I left my car in the Galleria parking lot and walked across the bridge over the San Lorenzo River. The river, like Santa Cruz itself, had been named by Spanish explorer Don Gaspar de Portola. At this time of year, sand bars and undergrowth choked the dry riverbed.

I took a shortcut, cutting across San Lorenzo Park where some of the homeless had already laid down their sleeping bags for the evening. Crossing the duck pond, I found the path in back of the Holiday Inn, which had been converted to student housing for the University of California, Santa Cruz. The normally packed lot in front of the County Buildings had emptied for the evening, and I hoofed it across the asphalt. I then jaywalked, or rather, jay sprinted, across Water Street to the office of Sloan's Investigative Services. To my amazement, a light was on and J.J. Sloan, decked out in charcoal slacks and a white dress shirt, was filing papers.

"Been in court all day," he explained, like he'd been caught doing something bad. "You have a message from your client."

"Rusty Mills?"

"Do you have others of which I'm not aware?"

"What did he say?"

"Says you haven't been returning his calls." J.J. frowned at me. "Wants a 'status report.'"

"I'm calling now." I had come to the office for that reason. Phil's information seemed pretty good. I plopped into the squeaky desk chair at our one desk and used the only phone.

Rusty barked hello.

I tried not to sound too excited as I told him about the mivacurium chloride. After all, his mother had been killed with it.

Rusty listened intently. "Is the boyfriend talking?"

The lack of reaction to murder, even by a tough Vietnam vet who didn't particularly like his mother, seemed cold. "Not at all. He's true blue to Chrissie."

I went on in a rush to tell him how I'd gotten a lead on Chrissie. She was with Jerry's mom in a lemon yellow Vanagon. Since the vehicle had been Phil's home, she'd described it from the tie-dyed curtains to the bead work dangling from the rear view mirror to the license plate number. "I don't think it'll be that hard to locate. She sometimes parks out by the Wrigley Building."

"That's okay," Rusty said.

"What's okay?"

"You've done a good job."

"Don't you want me to pursue this? This girl *killed* your mother."

"I've been looking over my finances, Carol, and I've decided I can't afford your services."

I shook with anger. I was being "let go."

I tried one last pleading effort. "If you don't care about your mother, how about invalidating Chrissie's inheritance? Isn't that what you hired me for?"

"Thanks for your help," Rusty said. "Send me a bill for my balance." He hung up.

I held the phone for a while, listening to the dial tone. I gently replaced the receiver. I turned and J.J. was inspecting me. "How'd it go in court today?" I asked to get his eyeballs off me.

He brushed his hands down his clothes. "I did my best to make Frederick look good and to make the neighbor look like a dolt."

"What's going on with Frederick?"

"His contractor neighbor is trying to put a restraining order on him."

"Because of our surveillance?"

"Nah." J.J. guffawed. "Frederick has taken to walking around nude in his back yard. He thought a view of his dick might discourage the neighbors from inhabiting their supposedly nonhabitable two-story structure."

"How can they put a restraining order on him for that?" All my indignation at Rusty slopped into my indignation at this other contractor. At the moment, I hated all contractors. "It's a private back yard."

"People can *try* to put a restraining order on you for anything."

"Doesn't Frederick have a hot tub back there?"

"Now, now," J.J. said, closing the file cabinet. "My appearance in court had nothing to do with whether Frederick has a right to let his wanger flap in the wind or not. It has everything to do with Frederick having a proclivity for private investigators and the means to hire them. You need to lose some of those scruples, Carol, if you want to be successful in this business."

I turned in the squeaky chair and looked around the grim office. This was successful? "Are you firing me, too?"

"Are you kidding?" J.J.'s smile revealed his big front capped teeth. "David's like a terrier. He'd bite into my ass and never let go."

I knew that J.J. had taken me on as a favor to David, but I didn't like it spelled out so clearly. I'd been told our bodies were more energy than mass, but right now I felt like a lump, a failure as a PI, as a baker, as a girlfriend and as a daughter.

"Frederick is easy to understand," J.J. said, leaning over me, opening the top desk drawer and extracting a small bottle of Jim Beam and two, not-so-clean looking shot glasses. "It's your client that I don't get."

Without consulting me, he poured us both a drink. I figured the whiskey would disinfect the glass.

He lifted his drink. "Here's to you and here's to me. May we never disagree. But if we do, to hell with you and here's to me."

J.J. knocked back the shot and slammed down the glass.

I managed half the bourbon and blinked hard against tears.

"Yeah, that Rusty I-hope-he-pays-his-bill-on-time, now there's a fishy character." He poured himself another drink. "He looked at the will with the family lawyer, right?"

I nodded. To try to win J.J.'s approval, I tipped back my head, gulped the last of my shot, and slammed the glass on the desk.

That was a mistake. As soon as the glass touched wood, J.J. poured me another. My face prickled with heat.

J.J. slugged down his drink. I sipped mine. "Presumably the lawyer helped the mom with the will. Wouldn't he have voiced some concern or reservation if he thought this guy's mother had diminished capacity?"

"Maybe he didn't care." The whiskey emboldened me. "Maybe the lawyer only cared about a paying client."

"Yeah, well, what kind of guy doesn't want to pursue a lead on a perp?" J.J. said. "His mother's killer for Christ's sake?"

J.J. insisted upon driving me to my car, but I declined. "Well, don't go off half-cocked," he advised me. "Anything you do now is on your own dime."

The evening air cooled my flushed face. The walk helped clear my head.

I no longer had a client, but I did have a mother who was probably awake by now.

My mother's eyes opened and she murmured hello, but it was clear we were not about to have a heart-to-heart. I told her that I was looking into residential care facilities.

One pale hand reached for me. "Harbor . . . View," she croaked.

That was the last place I wanted to send her. I patted the dry, bony hand. "We need to find a *good* facility where you can recover with assistance and then live independently when you're back on your feet."

My mother tried to say something. "You . . . ." She sounded like a frog.

I leaned in close to her pale face.

" . . . smell . . . like . . . booze."

I couldn't help myself. I said, "I've been drowning my sorrows in alcohol, Mom."

She glared at me and then shut her eyes.

After five minutes of watching her sleep, I felt like I did on those occasions as a child when my brother Donald had an event and my mother had been unable to force me to go. Left alone in the house, I'd been free to explore places like the back of my mother's closet or under my brother's mattress.

There wasn't much to investigate in the room, however, just two bouquets of flowers, neither of them from me. I was truly a stinking, rotten daughter. Both were mixed bouquets, one garden flowers; a person didn't want to seem too romantic with roses or too funereal with mums.

The first bouquet was from the folks at Hinds House where my mom lived. I read each of their wishes for a speedy recovery and claims they would be thinking of her.

I admired the second bouquet before reading the card. The arrangement was not from a florist. Someone was a great gardener—snapdragons, sprigs of lavender, daisies. The second card said: Get well soon. Sally Motha (Nurse from Harbor View Estates).

The hair of my forearms crackled with electricity. This woman was entirely too interested in my mom.

CHAPTER 33

The nurse did not exactly tell me I had to go, but she stood with her big arms akimbo and announced, "Visiting hours is over."

I didn't sleep any better at home than I would have in the hospital chair. Possibly worse. Visions of Nurse Motha floating down the hallway of the hospital filled my head. She carried a gigantic syringe, long as a spear, and headed toward my mom's room. She got hung up trying to get the hypodermic through the doorway, but it was only a matter of time until she angled it right.

I woke in a sweat. Why hadn't I realized Nurse Motha didn't have to work at the hospital to walk into my mother's room? She could, like anyone else, enter the room as a visitor. Furthermore, she might even work there. I'd asked the nurse whether the hospital used employees from the VNA, but I'd forgotten to ask if they ever used a registry.

I tried to calm myself. Why would Nurse Motha want to kill my mom? *Because she's an insane murderer who already killed Mildred Levine and Gladys Mills. Who better to inject a lethal dose?* There didn't have to be any logical reason for killing. Some people had screws loose.

And there could be a logical reason for the nurse to kill. Maybe she had been responsible for Mildred Levine's death, not through murder, but through errors of judgment or neglect, and the chatty Gladys knew too much. Even in that scenario, though, the nurse didn't pose any threat to my mom.

Lola was nestled against my leg. I reached down to pet her and she startled awake with a, "Meep." She revved up the therapy purrs and I relaxed. My imagination was running away with me. In spite of what the old folks said, I'd seen no evidence Nurse Motha was anything but a helpful person, ready to rush to the aid of a stranger like my mom or a snot like Chrissie. It wasn't that odd that she'd taken my mom some flowers. And, if she was going to kill her, why wouldn't she have done it then?

Besides, the evidence didn't point to the nurse as Gladys Mills' killer. No, my suspect was a little assistant with a drug problem, about to inherit a million dollar house, who had gotten her hands on what amounted to a smoking gun. Tomorrow I would find her, and I didn't care if it was on my own dime.

The fragrance of Juicy Fruit used to scent the light industry area around the Wrigley Building, but last year, Wrigley had pulled up stakes in Santa Cruz. I circled the area, down Mission Street Extension, along Swift to Haut Surf and Sail, and then down broad Delaware Avenue. Vans and campers and Pace Arrows dotted its flanks.

Vehicle dwellers often parked here. The businesses closed at night and on the weekends, and the streets were quiet, away from public and police scrutiny, with no camp site fees, and the Homeless Garden was nearby where Alice would have access to a toilet and some work if she wanted it.

It was a warm day and the interior of my car baked. I yawned, tired from a restless night.

I drove up Natural Bridges Drive, and repeated my cruise around the huge block, which enclosed a field of nineteen or twenty acres along with warehouses and businesses. Alice's yellow vehicle should stand out like a gigantic sunflower.

On this loop, I continued further along Delaware. To the

left was Natural Bridges State Park where the monarch butterflies munched milkweed, hatched and hung on the eucalyptus in clumps of thousands until the weather warmed and they exploded into the air, gliding and dipping wonders of black and orange.

The road dead-ended at the Marine Lab's acreage and I turned up Shaffer Road to the Homeless Garden Project.

This street, too, was filled with vehicles that served as mobile homes, but there was no sign of a bright yellow Vanagon.

I pulled on to the dirt shoulder of the road, glad for my small, beat up Ghia. I would feel awkward and intrusive showing up here in a sleek BMW. I fished the bright red package from the top of the jumble in the back of my car. I was proud of the wrapping job over the Cheerio's box, the wide white ribbon tied into a perfect bow. I'd written "Alice" in a fine flourish on the envelope tucked under the ribbon.

The Homeless Garden included a ramshackle potting shed, green house, a building that might have served as an office, a portable toilet, and rows and rows of hardy, late blooming flowers—mums and daisies, statice and sunflowers. Sandwiched in between the flowers were rows of vegetables—flourishing zucchini, and tomatoes on their last legs.

Birds dive-bombed the sprinklers. There were two guys working in the fields, but they let me poke around for several minutes before one of them approached me. He was at least six foot four and skeletally thin, the bone structure of his face easy to trace even with his parched, leathery skin. Salt and pepper hair tangled to his shoulders.

"Can I help you?" He had one visible misshapen yellow tooth.

Former heroin addict, I guessed.

"I'm looking for Alice."

The briefest smile told me he knew her, but he suspiciously squinted his eyes. "Alice who?"

"Alice Stewart," I said without hesitation, although she might have been Alice Lone Wolf for all I knew.

"Why do you want to find her?" Like a bloodhound, he sniffed me up and down to see if I carried the reek of a cop or parole officer or unwanted social worker, the smell of old coffee and musty office.

I nodded at the package. "Birthday present. It's her thirty-eighth birthday this week. I don't know where, exactly, she's parked."

He didn't say anything. He turned, stalked down the row along the mums, and consulted with the other tall, rangy worker. The guy instantly looked over at me. After years of flying under the radar, avoiding the police, lying to the family, stealing to support a habit, sizing up dealers, and hiding out, they were naturally suspicious people.

I played with the ribbon, trying to look demure and innocent.

The man stomped back along the row of white mums. "How do you know Alice?" he demanded.

"Went to high school together."

"What's your name?"

"Carol Sabala."

"Carol." He scratched his head. "I think I heard Alice talk about you."

Not very likely, I thought.

His street smart side warred with the natural, civilized instinct that wanted to help out a nice looking woman holding a birthday present.

"You know Tracy?"

"Alice has mentioned her," I lied, wrinkling my forehead in uncertainty.

"The artist," he prompted.

"I'm not sure."

"She has one of those studios off Mission Street Extension.

It's around in the back. She lets Alice park there."

"Thanks."

"Tell her happy birthday from me."

"Sure," I said, walking to my car, although I didn't even know his name.

The artists' studios were located in defunct two-story warehouses of corrugated steel surrounded by chain link fence. The Ghia crunched and spit over the surface of the huge sandy gravel lot. The place was nearly devoid of cars.

The yellow van was parked in the back, the top popped up. How could David complain that my place was too small; it was palatial compared to this space where Alice lived with a kid. And how about when Alice had four children?

I pulled up in front of a studio and walked toward the van. I was familiar with this model. It was a seats-six-sleeps-four vehicle with a flip-up table.

No one was visible in the cab. The tie dye curtains were drawn, but the side door was open about a foot. I rapped on the metal. "Hello, anyone home?"

I stuck my head in a bit. The table had been converted to a bed covered with rumpled Mickey Mouse sheets. A slender leg dangled off the side. It was white and very still.

CHAPTER 34

Where was my mother when I needed her with her breathing mask and calm efficiency? My heart hammered as I climbed into the van. It was stuffy and smelled bad, but I wasn't sure whether from general circumstances or from the body.

The girl was surely dead. Her skin was blue-tinged, cyanosis, the result of deficient oxygenation of the blood. I rummaged in my purse, feeling the Colt, safely carried with an empty chamber under the hammer. I extracted a pencil and used the tip to lift the eyelids, making a mental note that I should carry latex gloves. Her pupils were pinpricks. The body smelled of urine, old sweat, and alcohol.

I pushed at her arm with the pencil eraser. It was stiff with rigor, meaning Chrissie had been dead at least twelve hours, but probably less than twenty-four. Where were Alice and her kid? I scanned the vehicle as though they might be hiding behind the bucket seats.

Beside Chrissie's bed was a kitchen set-up, a small refrigerator under a counter and hot plate above. They must have had electricity at times. There was no apparent note, but a pill bottle stood conveniently on the counter. I stooped to read its label. The prescription for Tylenol with codeine came from Stewart's Pharmacy and was written for one Harriet McGruder.

Jerry could have lifted the drug from the pharmacy or Chrissie from Harbor View Estates. This looked like a drug overdose, but not an intentional one. Chrissie was not the type to leave the world without youthful melodrama, some final recriminations or self-pity, or a list of reasons she shouldn't be found guilty of Gladys's murder.

Chrissie wore the same mini-skirt and puke-stained shirt I'd seen her in on Saturday night. No style maven would want to be found this way. Chrissie would have broken down and even made the bed so that she'd look good in case she made the local news. Suicide was out.

Guilt hung in the air like the dust motes. What if I hadn't let Rusty put me off? What if I hadn't sat around drinking with J.J. Sloan? What if I'd continued my pursuit of Chrissie last night?

I reached over Chrissie and used the pencil to slide open a set of tie-dyed curtains that matched those in the windows. A sleeping bag stretched the width of the van. Above the bag and below the windows, narrow shelves held the boy's life—folded jeans, tees, socks, and a Giants sweatshirt, a Walkman and a short stack of school texts and a binder. In the corner rested a baseball bat, glove and ball, and on the ceiling he'd taped a poster of Barry Bonds.

An inmate in a shared six by ten had more space. I returned the curtain, welling with anger at the absent Alice. What was life like for this kid? How many baseball games had he missed because his mother decided to haul him across the country to a Dead concert? Alice had apparently missed the chapter about sacrifice in parenting.

The van might have seemed like a snug sanctuary to a kid in Somalia, but in the United States, you'd hardly invite friends for a sleep over. Phil had reason to be bitter.

I backed away from the body and climbed from the van. I drew a deep breath of fresh air, but the long, tenacious fingernails of guilt dug into my shoulders. Another young girl dead and my fault. If I'd only been a little smarter, a little more persistent,

a little more like a real private detective, Chrissie might be alive.
I pounded on one studio door after another. It was midday
on a Tuesday. The artists must have been at their paying jobs.
At that moment I decided that in my profession I would need
to get over my hatred of cell phones.

At the fifth door, a woman answered. Her gray hair looked
wilder than Einstein's and she was dressed in her pajamas—
pink and gray striped flannel shorts and tank. She squinted at
me and picked sleep from her eyes. "Yeah?"

"Do you have a phone I could use?"

"A phone you could use?" she squawked.

"There's a dead girl in the parking lot," I explained.

The day ranked in my Top Ten Worst Days. It fell below
my brother Donald's death and it wasn't as bad as the evening
an asshole shot through the sliding glass door of my bedroom
and blew off Lola's tail, but it was bad. Three squad cars arrived
almost in unison, and one of the officers called his sergeant to
the scene. And someone called the coroner. Standing in the
sun, a uniformed cop grilled me until a detective also arrived
and grilled me all over again, keeping me at a distance from the
van which was being photographed and dusted. I may as well
have been in an interrogation room with a bare bulb glaring
down at me.

The officer and detective seemed fixated on how to find
Alice Stewart, the owner of the vehicle. Since I'd come to the
van, they didn't believe I'd never met Alice Stewart and had no
idea how to locate her.

I told the detective how I'd been hired by Rusty Mills to
find Chrissie. The mention of J.J. Sloan's name made him smile
secretly to himself, but he didn't comment.

I told him about Gladys Mills and her will and Rusty's
unhappiness, but I held back my thoughts on mivacurium
chloride and murder. No one had hired me to investigate that.

No one even believed there had been a murder. And if the perpetrator were now dead, what would be accomplished by sharing my ideas except greater shame and big problems for the likable Mr. and Mrs. Stewart?

I could have directed the police to the Stewarts, but they'd make the connection soon enough, and the Stewarts wouldn't have any information for them, anyway.

I glimpsed the body bag slung with a thump from one van into the back of another.

I overheard one of the other uniforms talking to Ms. Pajamas who knew nothing. She didn't know Alice or her kid or Chrissie; she hadn't paid any attention to the van, didn't see anyone coming or going . . . .

When the cops released me, I bee-lined across town at a zippy thirty miles per hour, growing crankier at each stop on Mission Street. Death stuck to me like my dried sweat. I felt clammy and dirty with it.

Although the van was being thoroughly processed, even the detective seemed to regard Chrissie's death as a pill overdose.

When I arrived at my mom's room, she was as white as paste, but the stent in her heart apparently worked; she was awake.

An elaborate spray of pink gladiolus brightened her room. They were from her brother Teddy and family, much nicer than I would have expected from the tightwad. I read aloud the message on the card, written by some clerk at the florist's shop. "Very nice," my mom croaked and feebly pointed a knobby finger at the other cards.

"Do you want me to read these?"

"Yes."

I read the cards to her and she smiled faintly. I saved Nurse Motha's simple "Hope you feel better soon" for last.

"Nurse Motha is . . . ." My mother's head lolled to the side and she started to snore.

I wanted to shake her and shriek, "Nurse Motha is what?"

I sat with my mom for an hour, thumbing through the same People magazine as last time. It made me sad that the magazine was exactly where I'd deposited it, that my mom didn't have more people to visit her. I gave up the idea that my mom was going to wake up and talk to me. I headed home with visions of a long shower.

The hot water had barely penetrated my thick hair when the phone rang. I hastily wrapped myself in a towel and walked, dripping on the hard wood floor, to the bedroom.

"What the fuck are you doing?" Rusty Mills screamed at me. "The cops have been questioning me for the last half hour."

I tried to explain about Chrissie's death as I patted my body dry.

"I know the cunt is dead."

I hated that word. I hated Rusty Mills. I wrapped the towel around my dripping hair and sat on the bed.

"The cops have been here, remember?" he snarled sarcastically. "Didn't I terminate your services?"

"Yes." Goosebumps prickled my naked body. "As a matter of fact, you did." I was bumpier than a rye cracker.

"Then why were you still tracking that girl?"

"It's a free country."

"You're like those Earth Love pieces of shit. Acting out of some high and mighty principles with no consideration for how your actions affect others. I'm canceling your retainer. Don't expect any fucking payment from me." He slammed down the receiver.

I forced myself to exhale, long and slow. I couldn't have felt sicker if I'd eaten bad shellfish. I'd have to face J.J.'s ire, and he would side with Rusty. What had I been doing? You didn't want to jeopardize a client. Piss off a customer. That was no way to run the trade. I rued the day I'd put on my big pants and solicited Rusty's business.

The only small positive was that Rusty would not be able to

cancel his retainer. J.J. Sloan trotted checks to the bank faster than a person could say "Bounce."

I jumped back in the shower to warm up, but the nausea lingered. J.J.'s potential wrath wasn't the only assault on my stomach. I felt sick about Rusty.

CHAPTER 35

After my shower, I drove to Stewart's Pharmacy.

A grim-faced Bernadette Stewart met me at the door. "Chrissie Locatelli is dead," she whispered.

"I know. I found the body."

"The cops just left a half hour ago." There were three patrons in the store so Bernadette Stewart continued to whisper. "Jerry is in the pharmacy. He's completely devastated. We've taken away his car keys."

"I need to talk to him."

She looked doubtful. "I don't know. He's crushed. I don't know if he can handle any more."

Perfect, I thought. *For eliciting the truth, there was nothing better than a crushed, devastated person who probably felt very, very guilty.*

"Chrissie was murdered."

Bernadette Stewart froze. "The police said she had a drug overdose." She folded her arms over her pink smock. Who was I to know more than the police?

I had to say something to remove this roadblock. "Did Jerry tell the police about the mivacurium chloride?"

One of Bernadette's fists pressed up to her mouth. "You think Jerry killed her?"

"No, no, no," I murmured. "Chrissie took an overdose of pills."

"That's what the police said." Her eyes misted. "I don't understand. I thought you said she was murdered. What is this about?"

"Someone forced Chrissie to take those pills."

"Jerry would never do anything to harm Chrissie," she said in a rush, forgetting to whisper. "He loved her so much. That boy cares about me and his grandpa. He really does. But he was ready to give us both up to be with that girl." She pressed both hands over her mouth, paralyzed by her thoughts.

James spied us through the pharmacy window, his face distressed at the sight of his wife. He left Jerry, hustled to his wife's side, and put a protective arm around her shoulder.

She looked up at him, her eyes pleading. She couldn't speak.

"What's going on?" he demanded of me.

"I need to talk to Jerry."

"He's just been questioned by the police. He's in no condition to talk to you."

"Did he tell them about the mivacurium chloride?"

"The mivacurium chloride?" James exploded. All three customers stopped shopping to look in our direction.

"I told her, honey." Bernadette's voice was a choking whisper. "I just didn't . . . I just don't . . . want Jerry to turn out like Alice."

James stood in stunned silence.

An elderly man approached the counter with a hand basket full of goods. He wore a creased dress shirt with black slacks hitched up his stout belly and riding several inches over sturdy black shoes. He stared dubiously at the three of us.

Mrs. Stewart sniffled, peeled from her husband's arm, and went to ring up his purchases.

"I don't see how that strange order could have anything to do with Chrissie's death," James Stewart finally said. "Mivacurium chloride is a neuromuscular blocking agent. Hardly the kind of thing one would take to get high."

"Would Jerry know that?"

James Stewart scratched at the bottom of his toupee, secretly tugging at it. "No. Probably not. Even if he read the words neuromuscular blocking agent, I don't think he'd understand what that meant, and he's not a druggie." James Stewart's arm dramatically swept around the drugstore. "All those products, I don't think he had a clue which ones were good for a high. Chrissie educated him," James said caustically.

"Yes." I paused to let the grandfather filter my agreement through his cloud of defensiveness. "And Chrissie had Jerry order the mivacurium chloride." I told the grandfather what he wanted to hear. "Jerry didn't know what he was doing. He was innocent."

"But why . . . ?"

"I need to talk to Jerry to know that."

The grandfather led me up two steps into the pharmacy.

Slumped in a chair, Jerry was industriously dry swallowing pills.

"Jesus Christ!" James Stewart leapt forward and batted the brown pill bottle from the boy's hand. Pills hailed about the small room as I grabbed the phone and dialed 911.

CHAPTER 36

The next morning, Eldon chastised me for coming to work. "You should be with your mom. The kitchen can function without you for a few days."

"If it functions okay, why do we need a second baker?"

At that point he broke the news. He'd rehired Patsy, a tattooed lesbian biker who used to work in pastry.

"I thought you were adamant that we needed another baker?"

"Patsy is good at baking."

"But she's not a baker."

"She's a good baker and she knows the ropes of the kitchen."

I was cranky from Rusty Mills yelling at me. I felt heavy with sorrow about Jerry Vargas's attempted suicide. If I hadn't created a situation that had taken his grandfather from his side, Jerry Vargas would not have had the opportunity to stuff pills down his throat.

If I weren't in a bad mood, I wouldn't be arguing with Eldon. It was pointless.

Eldon knew that, too, and he left the room without comment. In spite of his nattering, he, more often than not, dealt with employees in exactly the right way.

I had mixed feelings about Patsy's return. It was nice to have some of the old guard back, but she and I had never been buddies.

During my break, I popped over to the pastry department

to say hi. Patsy looked the same except that she'd grown hair. Brown curls poked around the edges of her chef's hat. With her tattoos and muscles hidden by her chef's uniform, the curls gave her the permed look of a Sixties housewife.

She locked me in a crushing hug. We were both happy to have a familiar face in the kitchen, and we did a brief walk down memory lane, glossing over the murder in Archibald's kitchen several years ago. However, outside our shared kitchen experience, we didn't have much to say to each other. Patsy was a hardcore, motorcycle riding dyke who belonged to a tight band of rebels where someone like me would never fit.

That morning I baked poppy seed muffins and white bread scented with rosemary. My shift ended at noon and by 12:05 I was zooming down the hill to Dominican Hospital. The hospital had a building for seventy-two-hour holds, but if Jerry Vargas was too weak or sick, he'd be in the main hospital. Since having one's stomach pumped could be quite a shock to the system, I figured he'd be in the regular hospital, and as I knew from my mom's stay, unless a guard were posted at the door, anyone could drop by to visit a patient.

I didn't stop at the information desk in case there was a restriction on visitors. Instead I bounded up the stairs and cruised the maze of hallways. As a normal, middle-aged woman, I was one of the least suspicious looking characters in this world. I meandered, peeking in rooms for several minutes.

A small Filipino janitor finally asked, "What room number are you looking for?"

I gave him the number of the room in front of me. "But I must be mistaken. I'm looking for Jerry Vargas." I gave a brief description.

"Down the hall and to your left. He gave me the room number. I cruised by Jerry's room and casually glanced in the door. Bernadette Stewart was sitting with him. He was propped up and they both seemed intent on an infomercial for Tybo.

I wended my way to my mom's room, but she was snoring softly. I placed my thumb on her wrist, but it failed to wake her. Her skin looked less pasty and more flesh-toned. I poked her arm a few times to see how quickly the color would return.

My mom had a package beside her bed. I lifted it. It felt heavy. I shook it, but there was no rattle. I sniffed it and imagined the scent of chocolate. I plopped in the chair and restlessly thumbed through the People magazine. After a few minutes, I walked over to spy on Jerry Vargas. In his hospital gown, he looked thin and vulnerable. His grandmother was still parked at his side. The Tybo commercial was still on.

Waiting was going to drive me crazy, a very short drive. I wandered down to the parking lot and sat in my car. Out of boredom, I twisted to the junk heap in the back where the phony birthday present for Alice rested like a maraschino. It perched on the black fabric that had been tossed over my head, a thin material, shiny and slick on one side, furry on the other.

I scrounged in my glove compartment, dug out my Swiss army knife, and used the little scissors to cut a swatch of the material. I stood outside my car and folded the rest of it. Then I killed time organizing the collection of stuff in the back of my Karmann Ghia, shaking out and rolling up my car blanket, digging out the flashlight whose batteries had needed replacing for the last year and pulling out two sweatshirts that needed washing. When I headed back to the rooms, Bernadette Stewart remained exactly where I'd left her.

My mom was not only awake, but had two visitors—Ida Walker and Jack Dorfmann.

Ida greeted me sweetly.

"Nurse Motha told us Bea here was ailing," Jack Dorfmann explained.

"How did you get here?" I asked.

"Ida drove us over in her tank." Jack let his cane clatter against the chair. I casually leaned back against the wall. Instead of trying his butt grabbing stunt, Jack hunched over and imitated Ida gripping a steering wheel with both hands. "Outta my way world!"

I wondered how funny my mom would find this. Her retirement to Santa Cruz had been precipitated by her driving into the Ferndale Post Office. She smiled wryly.

Ida had brought my mother a book of crosswords and Jack had brought her a box of chocolates.

"Now we don't want those to melt," my mom said weakly.

"I couldn't agree more." Jack ripped off the wrapping and passed around the box. Although not a sweets lover, I took one to be polite.

While delighted that my mom had company, I anticipated the worst. At this rate, my mom would insist upon Harbor View Estates, and who was I to say no. The events of my life had forced me to recognize my own loneliness. Companionship would go a long way to compensate for drinking Tang instead of juice.

When the initial hubbub died down, I extracted the black swatch from my purse. "Do any of you guys recognize what this is?"

Jack snatched the black square and rubbed it between his gnarled fingers. "Tthathh," he said around a mouthful of chocolate. His fourth, to be exact. "Damn caram . . . ma. . .al." He plopped into the chair in frustration and used a knobby finger to clear caramel from his gums.

Ida reached for the fabric, but Jack jealousy balled it into his fist. "This is landscaping fabric," he announced. "People put it under topsoil. It lets water drain down, but prevents weeds from growing up."

Landscaping fabric. I imagined that Phil and Jerry's bald friend could work for a landscaping firm, but that wasn't the first person who jumped to mind.

CHAPTER 37

In spite of the mild weather, I pulled on my jeans and added a flannel shirt over my tee. I hitched my hair into a ponytail.

It had taken me until mid-afternoon to find Jerry alone, but the rest had been simple. As soon as I entered the room, he talked.

"Chrissie didn't kill Gladys," he said grimly. "I know she didn't." The boy was paler than my mother, the scoops below his jade green eyes almost black.

I turned off the television and sat in the chair, still warm from his grandmother's vigil.

"She intended to," I said.

"Maybe," he croaked hollowly.

"She didn't want that mivacurium for fun, Jerry."

"I didn't know," he stammered. "I only found out afterward. But she didn't do it. She told me she didn't. And Chrissie would never lie to me."

"*What a complete dupe,*" I thought.

"Afterwards she told me how Gladys said she was getting a house, and the way she wanted our life to be with a place of our own . . . ." He gazed down at his sheet. "With a home."

The last word reverberated in my heart. Yes, a home. For the first time, I believed the two might have really loved each other, pulled together in a yearning for a home, a stationary, secure center for their lives.

"What happened?"

"Chrissie doesn't know." A tear leaked down his cheek. "Didn't know," he corrected himself. "She freaked out and left the stuff on the kitchen counter." He glanced up meekly. "In Gladys's room. She went outside to take a break and when she came back, Gladys was dead and the stuff was gone. She was terrified."

Jerry didn't grasp his girlfriend had coldly planned to murder an old lady who trusted her. It mattered to him only that she hadn't done it and that she'd been frightened.

It took a really honest person to be such a gullible sap. I should know, but Chrissie's death left no doubt Jerry was telling the truth.

And even though Jerry had been Chrissie's marionette, in this instance she had not lied to him. Chrissie had set out to kill Gladys Mills, but someone else had finished the job.

"Did you tell the police about the mivacurium?"

He shook his head. Of course not. They hadn't asked about it and volunteering the information would only get him in trouble, his grandparents in trouble, and Chrissie, if she weren't dead, in a heap of trouble.

"Did you tell them that Chrissie was hiding out with your mom, that she was afraid of someone?"

He bobbed his head and wiped away tears with the back of his hand.

"Do you think Chrissie overdosed?"

He chewed his lip. "That's what the police said," he mumbled.

"Is that what you believe?"

He shrugged his shoulders and played with his white bedding. "What else can I believe?" he asked.

"How about this? Chrissie was being pursued. By the person who killed Gladys Mills. That person tracked her down and forced her to take those pills."

The kid stared at me—bug eyed.

"But if you don't tell the police about Chrissie and what she planned to do, I'll never be able to make this case."

I left him to ponder his dilemma. *Would he rather have his girlfriend known as a murderer, or have the murderer of his girlfriend known?*

Now, in my home office, I pulled my will from the file cabinet. I'd made the will using a book from Nolo Press. There it was, the typical, will language. I'd left the house to my mom, "or if she doesn't survive me by 45 days" to my former husband Chad.

I was willing to bet that if Chrissie didn't survive Gladys by forty-five days, that her share of the estate reverted to Rusty. After he had discovered he didn't inherit and a civil case looked less than promising, what was a poor boy to do?

I'd been played for a fool. A patsy. Worse than Jerry Vargas. At least he was all of about nineteen and had been raised by a woman who'd never grown up. What was my excuse?

I pulled my gun from my purse. Five rounds in the cylinder and the empty under the hammer. I could hear J.J.'s sarcastic voice in my head, "Now, now, Carol. Shooting a customer. That is definitely bad for business."

In my fantasy, I replied, "He's not going to pay me."

"Oh, well in that case," J.J. would say, smiling with his big false teeth.

I held the gun at arm's length, supporting the butt and my right hand with the left. The old gunslingers were always pictured firing with the revolver held straight out in one hand. Maybe because they fired from horseback and needed the other hand for the reins? Or maybe they thought two hands were for sissies. I wondered how they ever hit anything.

Even with both hands, holding my gun was difficult. My palms were swollen and stiff from landing on the pavement. The pain fueled my resolve. I pointed the gun at my file cabinet.

If I had to point it at a person, would my hands tremble like they were now? Maybe I should have opted for a bigger, more intimidating semi-automatic.

I returned the Colt to my purse. The revolver had been the police handgun choice for sixty years, until the firepower on the streets forced them into more serious weaponry. The average social encounter required 1.8 shots. I remembered that from my Criminal Justice classes.

I stroked Lola. "Bye, bye, sweet kitty." I should make a new will. My current one left Lola to Suzanne, but Suzanne was in Kuwait. If Suzanne didn't survive me, Lola went to my mom. But my mom was no cat lover and my mom could kick at any moment.

I ventured into the mild autumn afternoon and sat in my Karmann Ghia without starting it. In the back was the neatly folded landscaping fabric. I'd assumed that the attack on me had been intimidation, to prevent me from following Chrissie, but now I realized the person had not wanted me to see his vehicle.

I inspected my raw palms. Injury added to insult. I started the car and drove to Live Oak.

The trailer was a business office. I didn't see any reason to knock.

Rusty was smoking, leaned back in his chair, his thick chest a wide easy target. His astonishment changed to a smirk. My fingers itched to draw my gun, to blast the cigarette out of his hand.

Rusty dropped forward and scowled. "I don't think this is wise."

"Murder is not wise."

"Murder?" He arched a gray eyebrow. "You have a vivid imagination. What murder?"

"Well, first the one of your mother."

"You think I killed my own mom?" He chuckled. "The

State can't even round up enough evidence for me to bring a wrongful death suit."

"It's very convenient how between me and the State you know exactly how much evidence there is."

He stubbed out his cigarette and crossed his arms over his chest.

His mossy eyes flicked toward his desk drawer, paused on my purse, and circled to my face. "If you were such a hot shot investigator, I wouldn't have fired you."

The trailer was hot as a sauna, but I shook with anger. "No, here's the truth." I pointed a finger at Rusty's face. "If I were a hot shot investigator, you never would have hired me."

He scratched his chin. He looked again at his desk drawer and I knew he wasn't just longing for a swig of Maalox. He had a gun stored there.

"The wrongful death suit must have been Plan B, after you learned you hadn't inherited a fortune. What a slap in the face that must have been."

Rusty didn't even flinch.

"But when a lawsuit didn't look promising, you went back to Plan A—inheriting. You just had to get rid of Chrissie. And that's where I came in."

I fixed my eyes on Rusty's left hand. He'd been in the military. Even as a medic, he would have been trained to shoot. How fast would he be? "You didn't need me to discredit the will. You saw me as someone you could use, someone who could supply you with information, keep you on top of your game. You didn't even need me to find Chrissie until you lost track of her. I guess I spoiled your opportunity to kill her at the party. That would have made a more convincing overdose."

He clasped his hands and stretched them over his head, daring me to draw my gun. "Is this the place where I'm supposed to break down and start confessing shit. You should go work for Hollywood, Carol."

"Let me tell you how the script would read."

Rusty sat forward, and clapped his hands together. "That would be swell. Let's hear it, Carol." He reached for the desk drawer.

I whipped out my Colt.

"That's the stupidest thing you've done yet." Rusty opened the drawer and pulled out the bottle of Maalox. He took a sip and smacked his lips as though he'd sampled vintage wine.

"It's no wonder you need that stuff." I lowered the gun. "You know, Jerry Vargas almost did you a favor yesterday."

Rusty cocked an eyebrow, lit another cigarette, smoked and waited. I recognized the method. I'd used it a hundred times. Wait and people will talk to fill the void. Even at this moment, Rusty was outsmarting me, using me for information. I'd never hated anyone so much in my life.

I slowly forced my arm to bend and to slip the gun back into my purse.

"That was very entertaining, Carol," Rusty said condescendingly. "But if there's one thing I learned from Earth Love it's this: You may know something beyond a shadow of a doubt, but proving it in a court of law is an entirely different matter."

CHAPTER 38

Although it was early evening, it never occurred to me to call J.J. Sloan at home. David swore J.J. did have one; he'd watched a Stanley Cup playoff game there. But I couldn't visualize J.J. eating a take-out meal parked in front of the telly. When I didn't find him on his usual bar stool, I headed for our office.

Night made the place even more uninviting. The hallway was dark and I didn't know where to find the switch. A glimmer of light from under our office door guided me down the narrow hallway. In some places dim light could be romantic; in our office building it served only to enhance the stench of mildew and old cigarettes.

J.J. Sloan sat at the desk. He was not drinking. He was bent studiously over our accounts. I could not think of worse conditions for telling him about Rusty Mills.

He jerked his chin at me, what qualified as a greeting on the street.

Since J.J. had the desk chair, I sat in one of the two folding chairs that we had on hand for the rare moments when a client came to the office.

When I didn't busy myself at some task, J.J. raised his head and said, "What's up?"

I took the bottle of whiskey and two shot glasses from the drawer and poured us each a drink.

J.J. Sloan raised his shot. "Two minutes ago, if someone had told me drinking whiskey with a beautiful woman would make me feel ill, I wouldn't have believed him."

"Chin, chin," I said, and downed the liquor without batting a lash.

J.J. followed suit, but didn't pour another.

He was ready to listen and I poured out my tale of woe, right down to pointing the gun at Rusty.

"Well," he said calmly, "if you're right about this character, I don't think he'll rat you out to the police. It's too bad you did all that work and won't get paid. Live and learn." He looked down at the red accounts book. "At least you didn't cost the office anything outright. And we did get the retainer."

"What about Rusty?"

J.J. Sloan jerked his head up. "What about him?"

"He's a murderer."

J.J. rolled his eyes. "Did you already forget my little lecture about scruples? The people who need our services have problems. We can't go around turning in former clients. No one will hire us."

I sat silently.

"This is a business." J.J. rapped his knuckles on the red book. "And Rusty is none of our business."

CHAPTER 39

David pulled his car onto a sandy strip along the Coast Highway. Waddell Creek rested in a dip of the coastal hills and was a popular place for wind surfers. I twisted in my seat and watched their colorful sails zipping over the white caps.

"It'll be warmer as we ride inland," David reassured me as he climbed from the station wagon.

The snakes of sand blowing across the highway convinced me to do all the preparation I could inside the car. I loaded the sandwiches, chips, patch kit, and mini tool kit into our bike bags and put on my helmet, glasses and gloves. When I tentatively opened my door, the wind caught it, yanking me forward like a sail. I shoved the door shut and walked to the rear to help David unload the bikes. Sand whipped against my bare legs and flicked my face.

"That guy is right!" he shouted.

The wind blew his words into fragments.

"Who? Rusty Mills?"

He nodded to avoid a mouthful of grit.

Without comment, I snapped the water bottles into place. As I rode out of the parking lot, the wind blew me sideways, but as soon as I turned into the entrance of Big Basin Redwoods State Park, the wind was to my back and pushed me along the asphalt trail.

In the foothills, the wind quickly died. David rode by my side.

"There's no evidence," he continued.

"How about the shot given to Gladys's shoulder?"

"Even if this Jerry kid comes forward and tells the police about the mivacurium, there's no evidence she was injected with that drug. Furthermore, anyone could have given her the shot. We've been over that before."

"But it was on her right shoulder. So if the person were facing her, he was left handed."

"Listen, Nancy Drew. There are a lot of left-handed people in the world. The nurse is left-handed. You told me that yourself. Besides, what's to say the person didn't stand beside Gladys and administer the shot?"

"What about Chrissie's death?"

He shrugged. "A druggie who ODed. The police don't think any differently."

"But what about the connection between the two deaths? A woman dies and leaves a million dollar house to a young woman who turns up dead. Doesn't that seem suspicious?"

"Okay. Then how about this? By Jerry's own admission, Chrissie procured the mivacurium. She intended to kill the old lady. What's to say she didn't carry through? Only a dead girl's word to a boyfriend she controlled. Jerry said she was afraid. Maybe she was afraid of what she'd done. Or of being caught."

I shot forward, pedaling furiously. I hated that story. I didn't believe that story. But it didn't matter what I believed. Rusty had been right. In the end, it only mattered if a DA had enough evidence to build a case.

After a very fast mile, the road changed to dirt, cutting through farmland and following the creek. David passed me and I rode for a while in his dust until I gradually fell back.

Unlike Nisene Marks, this trail gently ascended, the farmland giving way to ferns, Douglas fir and redwoods. This was my favorite ride, but I plodded along, unable to enjoy the burbling water. Rusty Mills had committed two murders, and he was going to skate on them both. By tracking down Chrissie, I had aided him. And the bastard hadn't even paid me.

David waited for me at the top of a hill. I stopped and gulped some water.

He picked up the conversation where he'd left off. "So you think Rusty Mills strolled into his mother's apartment to visit, spotted this mivacurium on the counter and thought, "Ah, ha. I think I'll kill my mom today?"

"Yes. I'm saying it was a crime of opportunity. Rusty's mom was a demanding old sow. He resented her and he needed money. He thought he was going to inherit. He walked in, saw the mivacurium. He was a medic in Vietnam. He knew what the stuff would do or at least what a neuromuscular blocking agent would do."

"Wouldn't he have worried about someone missing the vial?"

"He counted on the person not wanting to take responsibility for leaving a potent substance unlocked."

"Maybe he realized from the get go that someone else intended to use it for murder," David said. "Maybe he saw Chrissie with the stuff. Why wouldn't he let her do his dirty work?"

"Because the stuff was laying there," I insisted. "If he had that realization, he would have known the plan had been aborted, that Chrissie had chickened out."

David sighed.

"Let's ride," I said. I pushed my shoe into the cage and pressed down hard. *Let him eat my dust for a while.*

David deigned to let me ride ahead of him for about a mile; then he soared by me. At the end of the trail, we locked our bikes in the racks, took our packs and bottles and headed off across the stream for a one mile hike to Berry Creek Falls.

A viewing deck perched right in front of the falls. We unwrapped our tuna sandwiches and ate greedily, watching the water spray over the rocks. Even at this dry time of year, the seventy-foot falls were marvelous, the gush of water soothing.

"I don't know how to get Rusty Mills," David said, throwing a bite of his sour dough roll on to the rocks. A Steller's Jay swooped down and snatched the treat. "But I know what to do about your mom."

"Oh, yeah."

"There are some good facilities in the area. Dominican Oaks just down the hill from your work, Oak Tree Villa in Scotts Valley, ..."

I cut him off. "She wants to go to Harbor View. She's made friends there." The jay emitted his raucous caw.

"Let me finish. Ida liked Harbor View because Gladys was there. Now Gladys is gone. You may be able to convince her to go with your mom to a new place. Shoot, you may be able to persuade Jack to go, too." He fed me the last corn chip.

A new place for everybody. It was an interesting idea. Not everyone clung to their little spot in the world the way I did. My mom had given up her house of almost forty years to move to Santa Cruz. And Suzanne had relinquished a hard-to-find granny unit apartment to travel with Hamad.

"I have full confidence in your power of persuasion," David said. "If one of those other facilities has three openings, maybe they could work a deal."

"I'm glad you have my mom's living arrangements all figured out," I said sarcastically. "But how about us?"

"How about us?" he echoed.

"Maybe we should follow the same logic and look for a place that suits both of us."

He was quiet, his dark eyes clouded. It was the right thing to do. Neither of us wanted to do it. We both loved our houses. The search for a satisfactory third house would require a monumental effort and a lot of time.

The water splashed, twinkling in the sunlight. It had taken time to etch its way. Even now it hit against limits, newly fallen trees and caved in earth.

"Time will tell," my mom would say.

With time, the water would turn rocks. Roll boulders. New surfaces would be revealed. A person didn't have to venture to Kuwait for that.

I hoped in time evidence against Rusty Mills would surface. I didn't see any more I could do right now if I wanted to keep working for Sloan's Investigative Services.

I'd learned from mountain biking that I had to look ahead and pick a trail. If I focused on the obstacles and ruts, I'd find myself in them.

I hoped in time David and I would find our path.